W9-DDA-572

Liam turned and walked toward the restaurant, so quickly and firmly she couldn't have grabbed his hand again if she'd wanted to.

Kelly followed him up the stairs and across the deck, the empty deck with its picnic tables inches deep in snow. He reached for the door, found it unlocked and pushed it open. They stepped into the restaurant. It was empty and dark. Chairs were stacked upside down on empty tables.

As the door clicked shut between them, a young man in a thick beard stepped out from behind it and pressed the barrel of a gun into the side of Liam's head.

"Down on your knees." The voice was low and mean. His face was lost in shadows and the click of the gun was unmistakable. "You're about to learn what happens to someone who tries to lie to Bill Leckie, and it ain't going to be pretty."

Maggie K. Black is an award-winning journalist and romantic suspense author with an insatiable love of traveling the world. She has lived in the American South, Europe and the Middle East. She now makes her home in Canada with her history-teacher husband, their two beautiful girls and a small but mighty dog. Maggie enjoys connecting with her readers at maggiekblack.com.

Books by Maggie K. Black

Love Inspired Suspense

Protected Identities

Christmas Witness Protection
Runaway Witness
Christmas Witness Conspiracy

True North Heroes

Undercover Holiday Fiancée
The Littlest Target
Rescuing His Secret Child
Cold Case Secrets

Amish Witness Protection

Amish Hideout

Military K-9 Unit

Standing Fast

Visit the Author Profile page at Harlequin.com for more titles.

CHRISTMAS WITNESS CONSPIRACY

MAGGIE K. BLACK

LOVE INSPIRED SUSPENSE

INSPIRATIONAL ROMANCE

If you purchased this book without a cover you should be aware
that this book is stolen property. It was reported as "unsold and
destroyed" to the publisher, and neither the author nor the
publisher has received any payment for this "stripped book."

LOVE INSPIRED® SUSPENSE

INSPIRATIONAL ROMANCE

Recycling programs
for this product may
not exist in your area.

ISBN-13: 978-1-335-57468-8

Christmas Witness Conspiracy

Copyright © 2020 by Mags Storey

All rights reserved. No part of this book may be used or reproduced in
any manner whatsoever without written permission except in the case of
brief quotations embodied in critical articles and reviews.

This is a work of fiction. Names, characters, places and incidents are either the
product of the author's imagination or are used fictitiously. Any resemblance to
actual persons, living or dead, businesses, companies, events or locales is entirely
coincidental.

This edition published by arrangement with Harlequin Books S.A.

For questions and comments about the quality of this book, please contact us
at CustomerService@Harlequin.com.

Love Inspired
22 Adelaide St. West, 40th Floor
Toronto, Ontario M5H 4E3, Canada
www.Harlequin.com

Printed in U.S.A.

Now faith is the substance of things hoped for,
the evidence of things not seen.
—Hebrews 11:1

With thanks to all the incredible women
I've had the privilege of teaching self-defense.

And with love to my amazing daughter
who never reads my stories
because she's busy writing her own.

ONE

Thick snow squalls blew down the Toronto shoreline of Lake Ontario, turning the city's annual winter wonderland into a haze of sparkling lights. The cold hadn't done much to quell the tourists, though, Detective Liam Bearsmith thought as he methodically trailed his hooded target around the skating rink and through the crowd. It was three days until Christmas and a few hours after sunset. Hopefully, the combination of the darkness, heavy flakes and general merriment would keep the jacket-clad criminal he was after from even realizing he was being followed. The "Sparrow" was a hacker. Just a tiny fish in the criminal pond, but a newly reborn and highly dangerous cyberterrorist group had just placed a pretty hefty bounty on the Sparrow's capture in the hopes it would lead them to a master decipher key that could break any code. If Liam didn't bring in the Sparrow now, terrorists could turn that code breaker into a weapon and the Sparrow could be dead, or worse, by Christmas.

Thankfully, his target had finally stopped all that darting-around and doubling-back nonsense he'd been doing when Liam had first picked up his trail. The lone figure hurried up a metal footbridge festooned in white lights. A gust of wind caught the hood of the Sparrow's jacket, tossing it back. Long dark hair flew loose around the Sparrow's slender shoulders.

Liam's world froze as déjà vu flooded his senses. His target was a woman.

What's more, Liam was sure he'd seen her somewhere before. Although in that moment, for some inexplicable reason, his brain had stalled so completely he could only pray God would remind him of where.

It had been almost a year since Liam's secretive team of rogue Royal Canadian Mounted Police detectives had taken down a cyberterrorist duo called the "Imposters" on Christmas Eve, to stop them from auctioning off the RCMP's entire witness-protection database to criminals on the dark web. Two of Liam's colleagues had been reluctantly forced to kill the pair. Their team hadn't realized for months that during the chaos, the Sparrow had somehow slipped her way into the Imposters's criminal auction through a hacked back door and deleted just one witness's file before it could be compromised. That file had belonged to a young woman named Hannah Phillips, whose military contractor husband, Renner, was presumed dead in Afghanistan after having developed a master decipher key that could hack any code in the world.

Now, the Imposters had been reborn, as

an all-new group of nameless and face-less hackers had taken up their mantle and hailed the original duo as heroes, vowing revenge on Liam's team. They'd placed a bounty on Liam's target, as well as being so determined to get their hands on Renner's master-key decoding device that they were threatening to cause mass chaos on New Year's Eve by crash-ing power grids around the world unless someone turned it over to them.

Liam's strategy had been to capture the Sparrow, question her and use the intel gleaned to locate these new Imposters. His brain freezing at the mere sight of her hadn't exactly been part of the plan. The Sparrow reached up, grabbed her hood and yanked it back down again firmly, but not before Liam caught a glimpse of a delicate jaw that was determinedly set and of the thick flakes that clung to her long lashes. She hurried down the other side of the bridge. For a moment Liam just stood there, his hand on the railing and his heart still praying for clarity, as his mind filled with the name and face of a young woman he'd known and loved a very long time ago.

Kelly Marshall.

Kelly had been nineteen and he'd been twenty-two when he'd shown up on her college campus, over two decades ago, to break the news that her father had been laundering money for gangsters and she needed to go into witness protection with her mother. Kelly had been defiant, spectacular and beautiful. In the couple weeks they'd been in each other's lives, she'd wrenched open his closed heart, made him question his will to be a cop and left a hole inside him so big he'd never risked loving anyone again.

No. It couldn't be Kelly. Not here. Not now.

She plunged into a crowded Christmas market on the other side of the footbridge and now weaved her way through the mass of shoppers and stalls. Liam strode after her. At six foot five, with the build of a bouncer, he knew it took far more than just hiding his bulletproof vest under a leather jacket to make him look inconspicuous. So, instead, he'd learned how to be invisible—a handy skill for the son of a prominent RCMP officer growing up in a working-class town like Kingston, where over half the kids in his class had a relative in jail. Liam thankfully didn't remember much about his abusive and unstable alcoholic mother, beyond knowing she was the reason he still sometimes flinched when people tried to hug him and why he had always appreciated his late father's focus on calm, rules and self-discipline over emotion and sentiment. Liam moved along the edges of the stalls with the steady gait he'd learned from his father. It was the kind that made people instinctively get out of his way and then forget they'd ever seen him.

His emotions swirled like the snow. He pushed them away and focused on facts.

The rise and fall of military contractor Renner Phillips was fascinating. A low-level computer analyst in Afghanistan, he'd suddenly thwarted a major terrorist attack after breaking a seemingly impenetrable code. Rumor was he'd developed a powerful decryption device. The government ordered him to turn it over. Countless terrorist groups placed him on their target lists, offering Renner bribes and threatening to hurt his young wife, Hannah, as leverage. For a few brief hours he was the world's most sought-after man. Then the SUV he'd been traveling in blew up. Renner was presumed dead, the decipher key was assumed destroyed in the explosion and Hannah had gone into RCMP witness protection.

Everyone had thought it was over, until this woman he was now following—who inexplicably reminded him of Kelly—had nabbed Hannah's RCMP witness-protection file from the original Imposters a year ago, and then these new reborn Imposters had threatened global chaos unless they got their hands on Renner's decoding device.

And Liam, for one, was tired of surprises.

He reached for his cell phone and hit the number of their resident tech genius, Seth Miles. The phone rang in Liam's earpiece. A former criminal hacker himself, Seth had spent most of his adult life trying to be some kind of vigilante, targeting bad guys and exposing their crimes, before he'd gone after the wrong guys and ended up in witness protection. Now, despite Seth's sketchy past and unconventional way of doing things, he was the only noncop on Liam's elite team. Seth didn't answer.

Liam hit Redial. Carolers belted tunes to his right. The smell of hot chocolate tried to yank his attention left. But his eyes stayed locked on the woman ahead, as she slipped from the stalls and attached herself to a small group of people now moving down the docks, as if pretending that she was with them.

Smart move, Liam thought. It was a tactic his father had taught him and that he'd often used himself.

His phone clicked. "Hey, Seth?"

"Yo, Liam." Seth's voice filled his ear. "Tell me you want to split the cost of three toasters."

Three toasters? Liam's eyes rolled for a nanosecond before he locked back on the woman ahead. As usual, Liam had no idea what Seth was talking about and limited patience to ferret it out. "Did you know the person who hacked into the file of deceased contractor Renner Phillips's widow, Hannah, was a woman?"

There was a slightly strangled sound on the line.

"Are you sure?" Seth asked.

"That Renner's actually dead?" Liam asked. He and Seth had debated this one more than a few times since the new Imposters had threatened global chaos if they didn't get Renner's decoding device. Despite all evidence, Seth remained doggedly convinced that Renner was still alive. But if so, what kind of man would just abandon his new wife like that and disappear? "Still no. Though I've got no intel to back that up."

"That the Sparrow is a woman," Seth clarified.

"I have eyes on her as we speak." The wood beneath his feet was slippery with ice and damp with melting snow. Now that he'd left the fair behind, all remaining foot traffic seemed to be heading toward a large, three-story cruise ship/party boat. According to the yellow posters taped to metal lampposts around him, it was about to set sail for the Ugly Sweater Holiday Cruise.

"What does she look like?" Seth asked.

Way too much like a woman named Kelly Marshall I placed in witness protection over twenty years ago.

"Five foot five," Liam said. "Long dark

hair. Athletic legs. About a hundred and forty pounds, but hard to tell in the ski jacket. No clear visual on her face."

"But how do you know that you're following the right person?" Seth wasn't letting it go.

"I got a tip," Liam said.

"From?" Seth asked.

"A contact." Liam kept from pointing out the fact that just because Seth hadn't been able to get a solid lead on her didn't mean no one could. "I know a lot of people who owe me one."

"How about you get me a picture and I'll run it through the system?" Seth suggested.

"Good idea," Liam said. "Stand by."

A good hard look at his target's face to prove to himself that she wasn't Kelly might not hurt any. Someone had helpfully left a bright pink mitten on the back of a metal bench. He picked it up and rolled it between his fingers, as his footsteps quickened. "Any idea yet which specific power grids these new Imposters are targeting on New Year's Eve?"

"Not yet," Seth said. "Have I told you I think it's a colossal mistake for law enforcement to try to keep news of this threat from getting out?"

"A few times."

But law enforcement tended to avoid leaking news of terrorist threats that could cause mass panic whenever they could help it. And "an anonymous mob of bad guys are threatening to do a really bad thing to unknown locations unless they get their hands on something powerful that might've been destroyed from someone who might be dead" was hardly reassuring. They didn't even know any of these new Imposters's identities. Only that they were young men who were angry, congregated online and had no centralized leader.

"You can't keep something off the internet forever," Seth said. "It's a cyberworld out there, old man."

"Duly noted," Liam said. "Any word yet on who the leaders of the Imposters are?"

"As I've explained, online mobs don't have leaders," Seth said. "They have lots of individuals suggesting chaos and others jumping on the bandwagon, with no one really sure who started it. Even if there was someone on the dark-web message boards posing as the big-bad-boss Imposter, there's no reason to believe he has any more knowledge or leadership than anyone else. Pffft, anyone could randomly call themselves the leader of a group like that and it would be virtually meaningless."

The Sparrow had stopped by a tree a little bit away from the crowd. It looked like she was on the phone.

"So about those toasters?" Seth's voice was back in his ear. "You know we got three weddings in ten days now?"

"Two weddings," Liam corrected. Two of the detectives in their five-person team were getting married over the holidays, both to former witnesses whose files had been compromised by the Imposters. Noah Wilder was marrying Corporal Holly Asher in two days, on Christmas Eve, and Mack Grey was marrying Iris James, a social worker, a week later on New Year's Eve. The team's year of dealing with the auction's fallout had definitely taken some eventful turns.

"Three now," Seth said. "Jess is getting married tomorrow at one."

"What?" Liam faltered a step. Last he'd heard, the final member of their team, Detective Jessica Eddington, was set to marry Travis Tatlow in the spring. "Everything okay?"

"She got offered a contract consulting on a special-victims unit in Florida and decided they and the kids should all go together as a family," Seth said. Travis had recently adopted two small children he'd grown close to while living in witness protection. "I'm really sorry. I just assumed she'd called you before me."

"Don't worry," Liam said. Jess and Seth had gotten close on a previous assignment, and Liam had never viewed his work as a popularity contest. "I'm sure she's got a lot on her mind and a lot of people to contact."

In fact, Liam could see Jess's name popping up on his phone now, but he declined her call, planning to congratulate her later. The Sparrow had ended her call and had started walking again. Her pace quickened, and he sped up to match it.

"So that just leaves us two bachelors standing," Seth said. "But I'm hoping if marriage is contagious it's only affecting detectives. Not that I think you'd be at risk."

"Uh… Huh?" Liam just grunted in response. What was that supposed to mean?

"You know, I read your file—"

"Don't read people's files—"

"—it's a great read," Seth went on. "Two decades on the force, over a gazillion arrests, but no significant relationships. No brothers or sisters. No family, besides your late dad. Never married. Never dated. Never fallen in love. You're practically one of those clay warriors come to life."

"I think you mean a golem," Liam said.

"Don't think I've ever even seen you hug anyone—"

"I'm not big on hugs." Or on Seth's usual nonsense. The Sparrow slipped her phone into her pocket. Liam was only a few feet behind her now. He readied his cell to snap a picture and then reached out with the mitten, tapping her arm as he did so. "Excuse me, miss? Did you drop this?"

She turned. Kelly Marshall's fierce green eyes locked defiantly on his. The delicate lips he'd once kissed parted in a gasp. Liam felt all the blood drain from his face. Seth had been wrong. Liam had thought himself in love once, with a woman he'd lost his heart, head and almost entire career over.

And now he was going to arrest her.

* * *

"Liam?" Kelly felt the name of the man she'd once loved slip from her lips. Shivers cascaded down her limbs as she looked up into the dark eyes she'd never imagined she'd see again. For a moment, she couldn't believe it was really him, or even if she'd said his name out loud, until she saw him nod and heard him say "Hey, Kelly" in that same deep voice that had always rumbled faintly like distant thunder at the edges of her memory.

Faded scars traced the strong lines of Liam's jaw and there were at least two new bends in his nose. Gray brushed the temples of his short dark hair. He looked both weathered and stronger somehow, and maybe a little tired. But despite the outward changes from both past battles and time, the intensity in his gaze was as powerful as it had always been. He lowered his head toward hers. His voice was deep and low in her ear. "Did you hack

Renner Phillips's widow's witness-protection file?"

So many questions flooded her mind that for a moment she couldn't find her voice. How did he know? How had he found her? This man who'd once convinced her foolish heart he loved her, and had even asked her to marry him, then had disappeared from her life entirely, leaving her to a life in witness protection, caring for a mother who was having a nervous breakdown, while pregnant with his child—his daughter, Hannah—whom he'd never even acknowledged beyond a terse email telling her to put the baby up for adoption.

"I'll ask you again," Liam said. "Why did you hack and destroy Hannah Phillips's witness-protection file?"

How could he even ask her that? Had he not figured it out?

"To protect her, Liam!" she answered honestly. "Because she's our Hannah! She's our girl."

Yes, the adoption had been closed, but their brilliant, beautiful and incredibly talented twenty-one-year-old daughter had searched for Kelly and found her after her adoptive parents had been killed in a car crash when Hannah was in her first year of college. When Kelly had written to Liam about the birth of their daughter, she'd told him Hannah's first name. Certainly Liam was a smart enough detective to match Hannah's name, birth date and the fact she was an adoptee to the letter Kelly had sent, years ago, telling him their baby had been a girl.

Behind her she could hear someone calling out "final boarding" for the party cruise. She glanced back. The line to board had dwindled down to a handful of stragglers. A thin man with a giant red Santa sweater over his jacket was yelling into a megaphone that anyone left had better hurry up. Hannah and her infant daughter were already on board, waiting for Kelly, so that together they could escape the cruise by motorboat, get into the United States undetected and finally reunite Hannah with her husband, Renner, after over a year apart.

A shiver ran down her spine. Did Liam know that Hannah had been pregnant with Renner's child when he disappeared? Or that Renner was still alive and had spent months in hiding, while working desperately and diligently to find a way to reunite with his wife, so the two young newlyweds could finally be together?

For her part, Kelly had both disliked and doubted the couple's plan from the start. Why not just come forward after the roadside bombing? Why had Renner instead gone into hiding? Hannah had explained that it was because there was no master-key decoding device, and that those who wanted to get their hands on it would never believe that was true, so Renner was doing what he had to in order to keep her safe.

It was clear that Hannah loved her husband and vice versa. The threats against their lives had been real and Kelly knew that Renner was a good man with a good heart. But they were both so young. They weren't thinking through their decisions. And Kelly's attempt to talk them into finding another way had fallen on deaf ears. Now all she could do was go with her daughter, help protect her and ask Renner what he was thinking, face-to-face.

Unless Liam had a better plan? Could Liam be an unexpected ally in talking their strong-willed daughter out of this plan?

"What do you mean she's our girl?" Liam's question drew her eyes back to his face. His tone was baffled, and his face was blank. "Who do you mean by *our*? Some group? Some crew? Are you somehow part of the Imposters or some other criminal gang that's after Renner's master-key decoding device?"

His words hit like a slap.

She's ours, Liam! Yours and mine. Our

secret daughter. The one we gave up for adoption!

She could feel the words forming on her lips, begging to be spoken. But something in the flat, emotionless look in his eyes made disgust twist in the pit of her stomach. Had he forgotten their daughter's name? The fact they even had a daughter? Or had he never read her letter? Either way, he didn't deserve her trust now. And yet somehow, as she looked up into his face, hope still crashed over her damaged heart, like a fresh wave on the shore. A horn blew behind her. The boat was leaving.

"There's so very much I need to tell you," she said, "and that we need to talk about—"

"And I want to listen," Liam said.

"But I have to go," she said. "Right now. Come with me, please, and I'll explain everything."

"No, Kelly," Liam said. "I'm sorry. You're going to have to come with me."

Liam's left hand took her arm. With the right, he pulled back his leather jacket just enough to show her his RCMP badge, gun and handcuffs. He was also wearing a bulletproof vest. "I'm arresting you on suspicion of accessing a criminal dark-web auction site and illegally accessing an RCMP witness-protection file..."

What was wrong with him? What had happened to the thoughtful, logical and caring man she'd loved a long time ago? The boat honked its horn again and the faint sound of party music filled the air.

The cruise ship was about to pull away, taking Hannah and the baby with it.

"Liam!" Her voice rose. "Stop, please, you're making a mistake."

He didn't even blink, let alone pause. "You have the right to retain and instruct legal counsel without delay..."

No, this was not about to happen. She had to go. *Lord, if I'm wrong, please forgive me for what I'm about to do.* Her hand darted to her pocket, yanked out a mini–stun gun and drove it hard into Liam's side, right underneath his bulletproof vest. He groaned and fell back, doubling over in what seemed to be both pain and shock. She shoved him hard, then turned and ran. Her feet pelted down the boardwalk, slipping on the boards.

"Wait!" she shouted. She shoved the stun gun back into her jacket pocket, yanked out a bright yellow ticket and waved it above her head. "Don't leave without me!"

Behind her she could hear Liam calling her faintly, as if forcing her name through pained lungs. The man in the ugly red sweater paused and she nearly crashed into him, barely stopping herself from falling off the dock.

"I have a ticket," she said and pushed the paper into his hand. "I'm sorry I'm late."

The man's eyes darted from her to what she guessed was Liam behind her. "What about him?"

"He's my ex," she said. "I hoped he'd

come with me. But instead he tried to stop me... It's complicated."

Twinkling lights shone and music thumped from the triple-deck ship ahead of her. She pressed her lips together and prayed hard. Maybe boarding the boat was a foolish move, but she had no time to come up with a better option. Hannah and the baby were waiting for her, and if she didn't go now she might never see her daughter again. The man nodded, took her ticket and waved his arm toward the boat. "Welcome to the Ugly Sweater Holiday Cruise. This party tour around Lake Ontario is approximately three hours long. The buffet is on the top deck. We return to Toronto at midnight."

And if her last-ditch effort to talk Hannah out of her plan failed, then Kelly, Hannah and the baby would have left the boat long before then.

"Thank you." She scrambled on board. People crowded around the side of the deck, huddled in winter gear and watching as the boat pulled away. She pushed through them and ran up a narrow flight of stairs to the second deck. It was only then she grabbed the railing and glanced back. The boat had pulled away from the dock. Liam stood there shaking his head, still on the shore, a few feet away from where she'd left him.

Had she really just run from the one man she'd waited twenty-two years to see again? How had he just let her go? But there was no sign of a police boat rushing after them or of anyone trying desperately to flag the boat to turn back. A jolly voice came over the speakers and welcomed everyone to the party. A cheer erupted from the deck below her and the music grew louder. What had she been thinking, asking Liam to come with her? Or hoping that he'd step up now after abandoning her and turning his back on her so many years ago?

She'd been a few months shy of twenty and happily pursuing a criminology degree with dreams of a life in law enforcement when Liam had walked up to her in the courtyard outside of class, flashed a badge and quietly told her to pack a bag because her life as she knew it was over. Less than an hour later, she was in the front seat of his truck as he drove her across the country to join her mother in witness protection, all because her greedy father had processed a whole lot of fake bank loans for some very dangerous people.

It had been a white truck, she remembered. Funny which memories had stuck and which ones hadn't. Liam had learned a whole bunch of handy tactics for staying alive from his father, and he'd shared them with her on their journey. One was that white vehicles were most likely to go unnoticed because they got dirty fast. Trucks were best because they were often mistaken for contractors and could handle tough terrain.

She hadn't thought of the introverted detective as her type at first. Liam had been too tall, too quiet and too slow to let her in or even smile. At first, he'd even flinched when she'd touched him. But she'd trusted him. He'd kept her safe when things had gone awry and the men her father had flipped on had ambushed them and nearly killed her. What should've been a two-day drive had instead ended up with them being on the run together for almost two weeks, with only Liam's quick thinking and the survival tactics she'd learned from him keeping her safe.

But more than that, they'd fallen in love. Or at least, she thought they had. Liam had asked her to marry him, she'd said yes and he'd promised he'd find a way for them to be together. Instead, after he'd kissed her goodbye, he'd never returned, answered his phone or even replied to her letters.

"Mom!" Hannah's hand landed on her arm as her voice snapped Kelly back to the present. She turned to see her daughter's worried eyes. They were the same deep brown as Liam's. "What are you doing out here? Come in where it's warm!"

"I could say the same to you," Kelly said. She looked down at the tiny baby huddled against Hannah's chest, so deeply swathed in a wool hat and coat that Kelly could hardly see her granddaughter. They called her "Pip." It was a placeholder nickname, as Renner came from a military family which had a tradition that a baby wasn't named until both parents had held her. In Alberta, parents had a year to register a baby's birth without penalty and normally that just meant waiting a few days at most. Kelly had no idea what Hannah and Renner would do if they didn't reunite before the year was up. "It's way too cold out here for a baby."

"I'm heading back inside in a second," Hannah said. She ran her hand down Pip's back. The baby was such a sound sleeper Kelly wouldn't be surprised if she slept the whole journey. "I just came looking for you."

Kelly glanced from her daughter back to the shore and suddenly realized how far out they'd gone. They'd already passed Toronto Island and the city's shoreline spread out behind them in a tapestry of shining lights. "Maybe I wanted to say goodbye to Canada."

And goodbye to Liam, too.

Kelly forced a smile she thought would look genuine but it did nothing to change the worry in her daughter's eyes.

"Are you sure you want to come with us?" Hannah asked.

"I'm positive," Kelly said. "As you know, I've got concerns about this plan. But that doesn't mean I won't go with you. I'll talk to Renner. I'll hear from his own mouth why he went into hiding and let people believe a decipher-key device exists if it doesn't. Maybe I'll talk you both out of hiding and into cooperating with the government. But either way, I'll be your mom and Pip's grandma." She'd rebooted her life once before. At least this time she'd be doing it out of love. "So what's the plan?"

Hannah glanced back over her shoulder, even though they were alone.

"In about twenty minutes, when we're closer to American waters, Renner says we need to head to a small motorboat off the port bow," Hannah said. "It'll be very small and pretty undetectable. He says there'll be a big, flashy distraction and that's when we make our move. He has contacts in the United States who've helped arrange for temporary visas if needed through an American contact. But either way he's got a plan to get us out of the US in hours and a new home set up for us somewhere in South America."

"What kind of distraction?" Kelly asked.

"I don't know, but Renner says it'll provide us the cover we need, and I trust him." A smile had crossed Hannah's lips when she'd said her husband's name. Now her daughter frowned as she searched Kelly's face. She was so observant, like her father, and practically impossible to fool. "What aren't you telling me?"

I just saw your father. He's a cop, he doesn't know you're his daughter and he just tried to arrest me.

As the words crossed her mind, she bit them back and instead prayed for wisdom. She'd had dozens of both excuses and justifications for not telling Hannah who her father was. None of them rang completely true and all of them came down to some variation of wanting to protect Hannah. She'd tell her when the timing was right— and it still wasn't right.

A tiny plaintive wail arose from below her. Little Pip had woken up. Immediately, Hannah started to sway from side to side on the balls of her feet.

"I've got to get her inside and feed her," Hannah said, her attention diverted. "I'm also going to call Renner and let him know you've boarded safely. There's a very small but quiet room on the lower deck that a kindly member of the crew said I could use. I've stashed her diaper bag and car seat there. This is supposed to be an adults-only event. Have you eaten?" Hannah searched her face as if to confirm she hadn't. "There's an amazing buffet on the top deck. You should go eat."

It was a good idea. Hannah probably wanted a few minutes alone to talk to Renner, and Kelly really did need to eat. She slipped her arms around Hannah, feeling the warmth of her and the baby between them against the cold air of the night.

"Go," Kelly said. "Get inside. I'll go get something to eat. Where will I meet you?"

"Bottom deck," Hannah said. "Port side. Twenty minutes."

"I'll be there." She followed Hannah inside, then headed up a narrow flight of stairs. Holiday music assailed her ears even before her feet reached the top. She pushed through a door and came into a huge room the width of the boat and the length of a ballroom, with glass windows on all sides. Gold and green decorations festooned the ceiling. Bright red table-cloths were draped over every table and went all the way to the floor. There were about two hundred people, she guessed, all clad in various Christmas sweaters that had everything from billowing trees to smiling elves and even giant bows on them. Hannah hadn't been kidding about the food, though. The spread ran over a dozen long tables covered with turkey, ham, breads and salads. Not to mention more types of cake than Kelly could count. She filled a plate, sat down on a very high chair at a tall table by a window and pushed some cheese around with the tip of her knife.

"Anyone sitting here?" The chipper voice was male and, from what she could see out of her peripheral vision, belonged to a tall man in a blue sweater with grinning jingle-bell-clad puppies on it.

"Actually, I'd rather be alone—"

"Oh, I insist." The voice dropped an octave to a deep rumble that seemed to move over her skin. She looked up, her eyes widening as Liam settled into the chair opposite her. Instinctively, her fingers tightened around her knife, but his hand dropped onto hers in a gesture that was no doubt meant to look friendly, but that kept her hand from rising off the table.

"Now," Liam said. "Let's try this again."

TWO

Music, chatter and laughter moved like currents around her. She sat there with the warmth of Liam's hand enveloping hers and her body felt momentarily frozen in place.

"Where's the stun gun?" Liam asked.

"Right-hand inside pocket of my jacket," she said. "Let my hand go and I'll pass it to you."

He chuckled. "That's not going to happen."

"Didn't think so." She wondered if he'd been expecting her to act all shocked and surprised by the fact he'd somehow materialized across from her on the boat. If so, she wasn't about to give him the satisfaction. She glanced down at their hands and couldn't help but remember how hesitant and uncertain he'd seemed the first time they'd held hands. The first time she'd hugged this big, strong man, it was like he'd never been hugged before.

"So you're just going to sit there holding my hand?" she asked.

Liam leaned across the table toward her. "I'm sorry, sweetheart, but you know I can't do that as long as you're holding a knife."

"It's a cheese knife that I grabbed off the cutlery table," she said, ignoring the fact he'd just called her "sweetheart," like he had back in the old days. Did he call everyone that now? Had he grown warm and cuddly, for that matter? Or was his brain misfiring at seeing her again, too? "It's pretty blunt."

"Doesn't mean you won't try to stab me with it," Liam said, with a smile. "Of course, if I disarm you of that knife you might throw that plate of food in my face as a distraction and go for the stun gun again. I know it's what I'd advise."

She could feel a smile trying to curl on her own lips and she gritted her teeth to stop it. Instead, she forced her fingers open underneath his and dropped the knife on the table, where it clattered loudly. She waited to see if it would make Liam let go of her hand. Instead, as she turned over her hand, somehow she felt their fingers looping through each other's just like they used to.

Clearly just a standoff tactic for both of them, right?

"I'm really sorry, but I do have to arrest you," he said, his voice barely above a whisper. "I don't want to make a scene and I definitely don't want to whip out my handcuffs. There are a lot of cell phones in this place and my colleague tells me the internet is everything these days. You deserve better than to have videos and pictures of your arrest plastered online."

Because of their past? Because he still cared about her? Or because a quiet arrest suited his purposes? She scanned the room. It was crowded, but she'd intentionally chosen a table for two that was set away from everything else. The noise and chaos around them would mean someone would have to be practically on top of them to catch a word that they were saying. Two people standing alone whispering in a hallway might look suspicious, but stick them at a small table, with their heads bent together, holding hands, and people would instinctively give them space and look away. She'd learned a lot about how to live without being noticed when she'd been on the run during her first two weeks in witness protection. Unfortunately, the person she'd learned it all from was the man now staring her down.

"Believe it or not, this is the first time I've held anyone's hand in decades," she said, convincing herself she was only saying it as a distraction, even though it was true.

"Me, too," Liam said and frowned. "And, no, I don't believe it. Now, here's what's going to happen. You're going to slide your stun gun and any other weapons you're carrying across the table to me underneath a napkin. Then, you and I are going to stand up, nice and slow, and walk hand in hand down to find the captain. I'll ask him to turn the boat around and drop us back on shore. Don't worry, I'll do the talking."

She felt her jaw clench. Sounded like he'd just accused her of lying. Her memory had generously edited out just how confident Liam was in his own abilities—too confident—or how irritating she'd found it even back then. She might not agree with Hannah and Renner's plan, but that didn't mean she was about to let him turn the boat around. Not until she knew Hannah had left safely to reunite with Renner, even if that meant she had to stay behind. As long as she kept Liam sitting here, at this table, talking and holding hands, then the boat was still heading toward American waters.

"What would it take to get you to let me go and walk away?" she asked.

"How about Renner Phillips's decryption device?" Liam asked.

Well, she appreciated the straight answer.

"I'm sorry," she said. "From what I've heard there is no master decipher key."

Liam blinked. "So then how did he decrypt the code?"

"I don't know," she admitted. "Fluke, maybe? He got fortunate and took a wild guess?"

One that had thwarted a terrorist bombing and saved countless lives.

Liam's jaw tightened. "But you believe he's still alive?"

"I do," she said. "But I haven't actually seen him or spoken to him, and I'm not going to lead you to him."

Liam snorted and leaned back so quickly the bells on his ridiculous Christmas sweater jingled. But his hand never left hers, and for a second she had to remind herself they were only pretending to hold hands.

"That's not quite how it works," Liam said. "He was a government contract worker. He had top-level government security clearance. He cracked a code without telling anyone how and then he disappeared—"

"Because a whole bunch of really bad guys had threatened to kill him and do worse to his wife—"

"Our government would've protected him—"

"He was targeted in a roadside bombing!" Her voice rose, not enough to be overheard, but still Liam's eyebrows rose. The music faded as one song ended. She held her breath and waited as the next song started up. Her eyes glanced to the watch on Liam's wrist. Whatever Renner's big diversion was, it was happening in twelve minutes. Which meant she had about ten left to ditch Liam.

"This isn't a game, sweetheart." Liam

leaned forward and something in his eyes darkened. "There's a really bad cyberterrorist group out there threatening to do some pretty bad stuff if they don't get their hands on Renner's decoding device." *Well, that was incredibly vague.* "The idea he took some wild guess on how to decipher some terrorist code and cracked it by a fluke it is frankly insulting. If Renner had turned his decoding device over to the government, law enforcement could've been using it all this time to stop these kinds of threats, instead of it being used as leverage. Renner needs to step up and help us stop these threats. We're not the bad guys here."

"That's twice you've called me 'sweetheart,'" she said. "Don't do it a third. And I wanted to go into criminology, if you remember, before you showed up and told me I had to go into witness protection—"

"Then help me find Renner and talk him into coming to work for us and letting us protect him," Liam said. "I'll pull some strings for you, too, and make sure you never see the inside of a jail cell."

Now she barely kept herself from snorting. "There's something going on you're not telling me," she said. "How are you even here?"

"How did I find you?" he asked. "Or how did I get onto the boat? A contact in Vice monitoring motels in the area happened to pick up your signal and tipped me off. And another contact in the Toronto Police gave me a stealth ride to catch up with the boat. I know a lot of people in various branches of law enforcement."

"Which contact just happened to have a big blue Christmas sweater with puppies that fit over a bulletproof vest?" she asked.

A laugh slipped from his mouth as if he'd tried and failed to stop it.

"Bought it off a guy on the lower deck for one hundred bucks," he said. "He claimed it was itchy and his wife was trying to make him wear it. Told him to take the money and buy his wife something really nice for Christmas." He stood up, holding her hand tightly and keeping the table between them. "Now, enough stalling. Slide over your weapons, otherwise I am going to very publicly arrest you."

She pulled the stun gun from her pocket and slid it across the table, as asked. It was out of juice, anyway, and she was sure Hannah would have a spare in Pip's diaper bag. She watched as he checked it, made sure it was off and then pocketed it.

"Now," he said, "we're going to see the captain."

"Wait!" Her hand tightened on his. Her boots dug into the floor. He stopped, but didn't sit. She'd kick herself later for what she was about to ask, but it would be worth it if it bought Hannah time. "Just tell me one thing. Why didn't you ever come back for me?"

Because if you did, if you'd cared or even read my messages, I'd have seen it in your eyes when I mentioned the name Hannah.

Liam's eyes widened and suddenly something soft pooled in their depths. A warmth? A sadness, even? All she knew was that it reminded her all too much of the man she'd loved a very long time ago.

"I... I tried," he said softly.

"No," she said, "you most definitely didn't."

"But... I did." He stepped closer, until they were just inches apart in the crowded room, and his hand was still locked in hers. "You—you were married."

"Married?" She yelped the word a whole lot louder than she'd intended to. Chatter stopped around them. Faces turned toward them. She didn't know if people thought Liam was in the middle of some kind of disastrous proposal or a shock confession about a previous relationship. But either way, they'd just lost the anonymity they'd enjoyed. Liam had noticed it, too.

"Come on," Liam said. He led her through a doorway and into a narrow hallway. Then he stopped, and for a long moment, they both just looked at each other without saying anything. She could feel her heart pounding so hard it ached. As she watched Liam's chest rapidly rise and fall, she guessed his heart was probably thumping, too.

"Yeah, you got married," he said. "I may be many things, but a gentleman is one of them. When I returned to the office and was debriefed after dropping you off, I was immediately pulled into a new under-cover assignment that involved total radio silence and kept me from contacting you. The moment I was out, three months later, I got hit with the news you'd married some man you met undercover."

"Married," she repeated. *What fresh nonsense is this?* "You think I married some man I knew less than three months?"

"We'd known each other two weeks when I asked if I could marry you," Liam said.

Yeah, and when she'd said yes she'd thought it meant something. Her heart was still knocking wildly. Did this mean he'd never gotten any of her messages? Did this mean he had no idea she'd been pregnant and they had a daughter?

"I never got married," she said.

He rolled his eyes, but more like he was in pain than frustrated. "And you never had four sons?"

"What?" She shook her head. "No!"

"Kelly!" Liam said. "Look, I'm not proud of this but I used to check your official RCMP witness-protection file."

"Then I'm telling you my official RCMP witness-protection file is wrong!" she said. "I never got married. I never had a son. Let alone four. And I wrote to you, a lot, in those first few weeks. Letters you clearly never got."

His nostrils flared. He let out a hard breath. Liam didn't believe her. He believed his own files and sources in the RCMP. A faint buzzing sound came from his jacket pocket. He yanked out his phone and answered.

"Hey, Seth," he said. "Yeah, sorry—before you say whatever it is you're going to say, I need you to pull an RCMP witness-protection file for me. Kelly Marshall. Placed in protection a couple of decades ago. I need to know her family status. Specifically spouse and kids. Yes, it's urgent. Yes, super urgent. No, I'm not going to tell you why."

He paused as if waiting for him to pull the file.

"Who's Seth?" Kelly asked.

"Seth Miles," Liam said. "He's a member of my team."

"Seth Miles," she repeated. "The criminal hacker?"

Seth Miles was either famous or notorious in online circles depending on one's opinion of vigilante Robin Hood figures who tried to do the right thing outside of the law. Did Liam have any idea how many laws Seth had broken? And yet he judged Renner for going outside the law?

"Yes, the formerly criminal hacker,"

Liam said. He turned back to the phone. "Okay… Okay…" She watched as he nodded and then nodded again. Then his face paled. "All right, call you back in a moment."

Liam hung up. His eyes locked on her face.

"Well, sweetheart, according to your official RCMP file, you got married three months after entering witness protection to a man named Robbie, and had four sons with him, named Robert, Gordon, Frank and Bill—"

"Well, that's obviously not true—"

He held up a hand as if to stop her. "It also said you died in a car crash four and a half years ago."

Liam watched as her face paled and her eyes widened. The fact that she was still so beautiful it knocked him sideways whenever he looked at her wasn't doing much to help his focus. Then she laughed. It was a mildly hysterical giggle that meant she found his information more unsettling than funny. Yeah, so did he.

"I can't believe I'm saying this," Kelly said, "but I'm not dead and I really did not get married to a man named Robbie. You can go find him and ask him yourself."

"I know you didn't." Liam ran his hand over his face. "And, no, I can't ask him, because apparently Robbie's dead, too. Your whole fictional family is. You all died in the same car accident."

Her hand rose to her lips. This whole situation was like a sick joke. One that his gut actually felt queasy over. He'd built his entire life around the integrity of the RCMP. The idea that someone could've deliberately falsified Kelly's file was unthinkable. A burst of cold air rushed in to their right, as a small mob of happy partygoers ran down the narrow hallway. Kelly pressed her back against the wall and he braced his hand on the wall beside her, placing his body protectively between her and the people pushing past.

As tempted as he was to get the captain to turn the boat around, this was also the second time in one night he'd been knocked sideways when he'd discovered what he thought he knew was wrong. Just how much didn't he know? The new Imposters had placed a bounty on Kelly's head in the hopes she'd lead them to Renner and help them get his decoding device, not that there was any indication they knew who she was in real life. *Thank You, God.* In fact, these new Imposters were so gung ho on committing the kind of major crimes they'd be able to do with a master key that could open any online door that they were willing to crash power grids worldwide on New Year's Eve.

And Kelly had just informed him that she was sure Renner was alive and there was no master decipher key. Hearing it from Seth was one thing. Seth had all sorts of crazy ideas. But Kelly?

What Liam needed most right now was information—information Kelly had—

and he'd learned in his line of work that sometimes it was better to keep a subject of an investigation talking for a while before arresting them. After all, some people tended to get pretty upset at being arrested and would stop cooperating, and he was fairly sure she'd be one of them.

More chattering came from the other direction now as a fresh group of people came down the hall, then more cold air rushed in. Then suddenly another fact hit him—Kelly hadn't actually tried to escape from him. That in itself was pretty interesting.

"I'm sorry I called you 'sweetheart,'" he said finally. "I won't do it again."

And he didn't know why it kept happening.

"Well, I just assumed you called everyone 'sweetheart,'" she said, as if trying to lighten the moment.

"No," he admitted. "Just you." He took a deep breath and prayed for wisdom. "Come on," he added. "You and I are going to go back to the party. Just for another quick minute."

Was it his imagination or had she barely managed to keep herself from sighing in relief?

His fingers looped through hers and they walked back into the party holding hands. He wasn't exactly sure which one of them had grabbed the other's hand first or why they'd decided to do it. But here they were now, and he was going with it. A couple of guys were sitting at their table, but without a word, they got up and vacated it when Liam nodded at them. Liam pulled the table closer to the wall and positioned the chairs to block people from seeing them.

"Sit, please," he said quietly. He let go of her hand and she dropped into the chair. He grabbed a clean red-and-green cloth napkin from a nearby table, spread it open and then slowly slipped his handcuffs underneath it, making sure she could see them.

"If I didn't know any better I'd think

you were about to do a magic trick with those," she said.

"And if I didn't know any better, I'd say you've been trying to stall me," he said. He sat so close her shoulder was almost touching his. "And I'd like to know why. Now, I don't want to take you out of here in handcuffs. I really don't. But you clearly aren't in a hurry to get off this boat, which is very interesting to me. So how about we play a game of twenty questions. You can sit here and keep enjoying the atmosphere, handcuff-free, as long as you keep answering. Fair?"

"Fair." Her eyes—strong, determined and full of grit—met his. She leaned her arms on the table and he did likewise. "So what aren't you telling me, Liam?"

A laugh erupted in his throat. Had she always been like this? He'd remembered her as tenacious and someone who challenged and pushed him. If she'd also been this irritating, he'd forgotten.

"The person with the badge asks the

questions," he said. "Starting with, how do you know Renner Phillips?"

"I met him through Hannah."

"Okay," he said, "and how do you know Hannah?"

Her shoulders rose and fell. "Pass."

"Why did you call her your girl?" he persisted.

"I called her 'our' girl," she said. "And the answer is pass."

"You don't get to pass." He clenched his jaw to keep his voice from rising an octave and his hands inched toward the handcuffs. Then he frowned. It was hard to tell with the darkness outside the window, but it felt like the boat had stopped moving. Was that part of the party cruise? "Who falsified your witness-protection file?"

Worry flickered in her eyes. "I have no idea."

And that he believed.

"Do you know why the boat's stopped?" he asked.

"No, I didn't realize it had." Her gaze

darted to his hands. "Did you really not get any of my letters or messages? Not even one?"

"No," he said, "I really didn't—"

"And you honestly thought I was married?" she asked.

"Yes, but—"

She grabbed his hands. "And if you hadn't thought I was married, you'd have done what?"

"I have no idea." He heard the faint sound of a baby crying somewhere in the crowd to his right. Not wailing, but just the small cry of a tiny infant trying to be noticed. Odd, he thought this was a child-free event. But between the question and the fact that Kelly's hands were on his, he didn't turn and look. He couldn't even remember ever having a woman suddenly try to grab on to his hand before and him not flinching or jerking away like he'd been electrocuted. "But it doesn't matter now, does it?"

Help me, Lord. I don't know what to ask.

He tried again.

"If you hacked the dark-web auction last year on Christmas Eve to prevent the sale of Hannah's file, then you've clearly heard of the Imposters," he said and watched as she nodded. "You probably don't know that three detective friends and I, along with a hacker, are the ones who took them down." At this revelation, her eyes widened. "As you probably know, the original Imposters are dead. Did you know a new group of Imposters have risen up to take their place? There's dozens of them, spread across the country. No known leader. They're threatening to crash international power grids unless someone hands them Renner's master decipher key. They also put a bounty on the Sparrow's head in the hopes you'd lead them to Renner."

"No," she said, softly. "I had no idea."

He searched her eyes. "I believe you."

"Do they know I'm the Sparrow?" she asked.

"I don't think so," he said. "I'm praying they won't find out."

"What are they planning?" she asked.

He left the question dangling for a moment without an answer. The baby cried again. This time he turned. A woman was heading out the door and onto the deck. Long dark hair fell over her face and her head bowed over a tiny little baby that couldn't be more than a couple of months old. Then she glanced up. Their eyes met. They both froze.

It was Hannah Phillips.

And then it dawned on him. *Oh, I've been a fool!* The party cruise would be crossing into American waters. As long as he stayed on the boat, he retained his full authority. But if either Hannah or Kelly slipped off the boat and made it to American soil, he'd lose jurisdiction to arrest them without an international warrant. He leaped to his feet only to feel something cold click against his wrist. He spun back in disbelief. Kelly had handcuffed her wrist to his…with his own handcuffs.

"No," Liam said, holding up a finger on his free hand. "I've been more than patient, but now you've gone too far. Hannah Phillips is not supposed to be outside Alberta without RCMP authority or have any contact with criminal activity. So being on a Toronto party cruise with the same woman who deleted her file is definitely suspicious. Not to mention she's supposed to report any significant relationship to her local RCMP contact, so if that's her child she's holding she's kept that tidbit about her life hidden, as well. I have no clue what's going on here. But I'm arresting you and detaining her for questioning."

He reached around in his inside pocket for his keys.

"Please, Liam, listen to me." Kelly tried to grab his other hand. "Let me explain."

Yeah, like that was going to happen.

His phone was ringing again. He stopped

fishing for his keys long enough to decline the call only to have Seth's voice unexpectedly sound in his ear, letting him know he'd just accidentally done the opposite. "Hey, Liam?"

"Hey, Seth, I'm sorry, I really don't have time—"

"Just got online chatter the new Imposters are planning some kind of major stunt in your area tonight—"

"What do you mean by 'my area'?" Liam said. "I'm on a boat."

"I know!"

Suddenly the doors on both sides of the ballroom flew open. Five young men in blue jeans, Christmas sweaters, black ski masks and colored eye patches stormed in. Four waved an array of semiautomatic weapons. One held a video camera.

Oh, Lord, please, help me now.

"Everybody down!" a masked man yelled. "We're the Imposter cyberpirates and we're taking over this ship!"

know he'd just accidentally done the opposite. "Hey, I—"

THREE

For an instant Kelly just stood there, her body almost paralyzed with fear. The world was a tableau of disbelief and confusion around her, as partygoers were momentarily too shocked to even scream, think or move. Then she felt Liam's handcuffed hand grab on to hers and squeeze tightly. And something, like the memory of once feeling strong and empowered, swept over her. Liam had protected her before. Not only that, but he'd also made her feel capable of protecting herself. He would again.

His free hand grabbed the table they'd been sitting at and hurled it at the men. Before it could even land, Liam had pulled her down to the ground and rolled with her underneath the closest banquet table. The thick red tablecloth fell like a curtain, sheltering them. She lay there for a moment listening as chaos erupted on the other side. A cacophony of voices shouting, screaming and barking orders clashed with the sound of more furniture throwing and things crashing. But, thankfully, there was no gunfire. She closed her eyes and prayed.

Please, Lord, end this before anyone gets hurt. Please keep Hannah and the baby safe. Help them escape this boat, even if it's without me.

"We don't have long," Liam whispered. "It'll take them a few moments to secure the ballroom and right now they'll be focusing their attention on anyone trying to fight back. Once they think they've secured everyone they can see, they'll start searching around for more. We wait for the right moment, then we run." She opened her eyes to find his gaze was locked on her face every bit as firmly as his hand held hers. "You with me?"

She forced her head to nod and a word to cross her lips. "Yes."

"Okay."

"Also, I'm—I'm sorry about the handcuffs."

"Don't worry," he whispered. "They're only number four on my list of problems right now. I can't reach the key from this position, but I'll get them off soon enough." Then he tapped his earpiece and spoke into what she now realized was a tiny button-sized microphone on his jacket.

"Seth? Can you hear me?" Liam's voice was low, urgent, and even right next to him she could barely make it out over the chaos filling the room outside their hiding spot. "Yeah, we've got a situation. Top deck. Five of these new Imposters at least. In pirate getup. Upward of a hundred and fifty civilians."

This was who the new Imposters were?

A group of heavily armed men in pirate patches? While they were masked, something about their voices and builds made her think none were much older than college students.

Liam turned back to her. She noticed he hadn't mentioned her or Hannah.

"Seth's watching the live feed now," Liam said. "It's all over the internet apparently. The Imposters say that they're cutting off cell-phone and internet access to everyone on this boat in six minutes, so everyone on board should get their final calls, texts and social-media posts in now. Law enforcement will take down their cell blockers eventually. Tactically it's a brilliant move. If everyone's staring at their phones nobody's fighting back, plus it's great publicity."

Oh, Lord, please don't let them find Hannah and the baby...

"Thankfully, I wasn't relying on the internet to get out of this," Liam said. "I always prefer going old school."

Old school. Like tossing furniture and hiding under tables?

"Who's behind all this?" she asked. "Who are they working for?"

"They're like a swarm without a leader," Liam said. "According to Seth, even if someone did claim leadership it wouldn't necessarily mean anything." He peeked through the curtain. His voice was low, quick and blunt, like he was giving a briefing. "No clear goal beyond getting attention and hurting those they think have wronged them. Imagine an ugly internet chat group come to life, in masks and colored eye patches."

He let the curtain fall and turned back to her.

"Our best guess is there are a couple hundred of them worldwide," he added. "Dozens signed the online pledge to take out their local power grids on New Year's. Maybe some of them thought this would be good publicity for that. Or maybe a splinter group decided to go do their own thing. Now come on." Liam tugged her hand. "We're getting out of here and finding you a better place to hide while I try to sort out this mess."

But her fingers dug into his.

"We have to get to Hannah and the baby," she said. "We can't let the Imposters get to them. If they wanted to use me to get to Renner, imagine what they'll do if they get ahold of his wife and child."

Liam's face paled as if his brain was suddenly recalibrating. "So the baby is Renner's child?"

"Yeah," Kelly said. She prayed hard for wisdom. "Renner and Hannah are still very much in love and a couple. He arranged for there to be a motorboat docked alongside this party cruise that Hannah, the baby and I could take to join him. Yes, I know the plan sounds stupid. Believe me, I tried to talk them into trusting law enforcement. But they're very young, very much in love, still seem to think they know everything and that it's them against the world." Liam, of all people, should remember what that'd felt like. "Renner doesn't trust law enforcement to protect Hannah and is convinced going into hiding is the only way to keep Hannah and the baby safe."

And the fact that her own RCMP file had been falsified was quickly eroding her faith in law enforcement's ability to keep Hannah and the baby safe, too. If her own file could be corrupted that way by someone inside the RCMP, who's to say Renner and Hannah were wrong to go it alone?

"If you get Hannah, the baby and I to the boat," Kelly added, "I'll personally beg Renner to contact you, explain everything and help you stop these new Imposters in any way he can. He loves his wife. He just wants to know she's safe."

The noise of voices and chaos was growing quieter on the other side of the tablecloth now. It wasn't a good sign.

"No deal," Liam said. "I'll keep you, Hannah and the baby safe. But I'm detaining you all unless Renner turns over his decipher key."

"There is no decipher key!" Her whisper rose.

"Then how did he decrypt the code?" Liam demanded. "And don't say he took a wild guess."

"I told you, I don't know!"

"My intel said—"

"Your intel also thinks I'm dead!" she interrupted. Was Liam really trying to negotiate a deal in the middle of an armed standoff? Just how many deals with criminals had he negotiated under fire? More than he could count, she guessed, just as she imagined a lot of cases had been solved as a result. But this wasn't any other case. "I need to explain about Hannah."

There was a loud crash and more people screamed. By the sound of things, the new Imposters had started searching the room.

"No time," Liam said. "Just tell me where she is."

She glanced at her phone screen, thanking God to see a message from Hannah. "Bottom deck. Stern. Small office room."

"Got it. Let's go."

He grabbed her hand, which was still handcuffed to his, and they slid out of the relative shelter of their hiding space. They crawled side by side, keeping their stomachs flat against the floor. Liam pushed through a swinging door and into a narrow and empty galley kitchen. Instantly, he stood, pulled her up after him and shoved a food cart against the door, wedging it under the handle. "We've got about thirty seconds before someone's brain registers the fact they just saw the door move and they send someone after us."

They ran through the galley into what looked like another food-prep room, then Liam rapped on the door of what she suspected was a supply cupboard. "Detective Liam Bearsmith, RCMP—everyone all right in there?"

Even hushed, his voice rang with an authority that seemed to crack the air like a whip.

There was a pause. Then she heard an older male voice. "Yes."

"How many of you in there?" he asked.

"Six," the voice replied.

"Anyone hurt?"

"No."

"Good," Liam said. "Stay there. Keep the door locked and don't open it until law enforcement tells you it's safe. Don't panic if the cell signal goes down. Rescue is on its way."

He led Kelly to another door, checked the hallway behind it and then turned to her. "Keys are inside my jacket, right-side chest pocket. I need you to grab them for me."

A large bang sounded somewhere behind them. Someone was trying to break through the first door. She looked back.

"Focus," Liam said sharply. Yet his hand was almost tender as it touched her face. Then he reached for his weapon. "I can get us out of here, but I need your help first."

She reached inside his jacket and her fingers looped through the keys. "Got them."

Another bang. Then the door behind them flew open and a masked man rushed through. The keys fell from her fingers. Liam spun around, placing his body between Kelly and the criminal, raised his weapon and fired. The criminal fell back behind the door. Liam scooped up the keys, grabbed Kelly's hand and pulled her into the hallway. They raced down it, reached the stairs, waited while Liam glanced to see if the coast was clear and then ran down. He paused on the second landing and his hand moved over hers— she didn't even realize he'd unlocked the handcuffs until they fell from her wrist. They kept running.

"Hey, Liam?" A faint voice crackled from Liam's earpiece and she realized it'd fallen into his scarf.

"Seth," Liam said. "Hey. Can't talk. Running. Update?"

"Law enforcement from both sides of the border are on their way," Seth said. "Helicopters and boats. They're currently in a holding pattern. It's all over international news. Internet's lighting up. It's quite the spectacle." Which she guessed was the point. "We're losing phone and internet in sixty seconds. You?"

"I'm with Kelly Marshall," Liam said. "Turns out she's not dead. Trying to locate Hannah Phillips, who's on this boat, and Renner's baby."

Seth choked out a cough. "You're telling me all this now?"

"It was need-to-know." Liam ended the call.

They reached the bottom deck, and after another spot check, stepped outside. Cold wind assailed them. Both the sky and water were pitch-black, dotted with the bright lights of police boats and helicopters that were keeping their distance for now. She followed him down the deck, but it wasn't until he stopped at a nondescript door that she realized he'd probably memorized the boat's blueprints before boarding. He grabbed the door handle. It was locked.

"Let me." She leaned past him and knocked rhythmically.

"Secret knock or not," Liam said, "she's got thirty seconds or I'm breaking the door down."

The door flew open. There stood Hannah, holding Pip in one hand and a handgun in the other.

"That's an illegal handgun," Liam said under his breath as if adding to the charges he could detain her for.

Hannah's eyes cut to Liam and narrowed.

"And if you make one wrong move," Hannah said, "I'll shoot you with it."

"Hannah," Kelly said. "This is Liam. He helped me escape from the party room upstairs. Liam, this is Hannah."

Kelly's voice was soft, firm and urgent,

and Liam couldn't help but notice she'd left out that he was a cop. His gaze rose from the handgun to the woman holding it. Nothing about Hannah Phillips matched the person her file had led him to believe she was. It wasn't just that she seemed younger in person. Since he'd passed forty and kept going, it seemed increasingly clear that people in their early twenties were half his age. But her file had identified her as overwhelmed, nervous and weak. One glimpse into her eyes showed a fierceness and determination that was anything but.

She reminded him of Kelly.

Hannah turned away as if she knew she was being analyzed and didn't like it. She slid the gun in her pocket. He took in the room. It was small with a short love seat, an infant car seat on the floor, a desk with a huge diaper bag on it and a chair that seemed way too big for the room. He watched as Kelly and Hannah hugged. Then Hannah eased the tiny little baby into Kelly's arms, and after a hug Kelly buckled the baby into the car seat.

Okay, and what is going on here?

"The internet and phones are completely down," Hannah said, "but I've hacked into the Imposters's feed."

"Excuse me?" Liam almost stuttered. She'd done what? Hacking skills had also been missing from his intel. Yes, Hannah's file had indicated she'd tested as gifted when she was young, but she'd also struggled through school and started a computer-related degree in college that she'd never completed. It was theoretically possible Hannah had taught herself to hack, but more likely Renner had taught her.

Hannah ran around to the other side of the desk and dropped the diaper bag onto the floor, and suddenly he saw the slim laptop she'd apparently been hiding behind it. Her fingers flew over the keyboard with a speed that rivaled Seth's.

"All crew and guests have been escorted to the third-floor ballroom," Hannah said with her eyes locked on the screen. "It seems the Imposters are gathering them all there. It's a slapdash operation. The call for volunteers went out on the Imposters's message board thirty minutes ago. 'Wear your own Christmas sweater and ski mask. Pirate eye patches will be provided.' They boarded the boat after the cruise passed Toronto Island, from a handful of motorboats they've now got all docked off the cruise ship. Now we've got eight hostiles total taking about two hundred people hostage. It's a complete logistical mess."

Hannah sounded like a cop. No, she sounded like him.

"Trust me, the boss Imposter isn't happy with it," she added.

"The Imposters have a boss?" Liam asked. Seth was sure they didn't.

"Not really." Hannah shrugged. "Someone stepped up as a theoretical figurehead a few days ago, but he seemed out of the loop on this one."

She spun the laptop around. Video of the room he and Kelly had just escaped from filled the screen. The camera scanned over the dozens of people sitting on the floor, then back repeatedly to an extreme close-up of a masked Imposter who seemed to be yelling directly at the camera. No volume.

"Any casualties?" he asked.

"No," Hannah said quickly, "or major injuries that I can see." He thanked God for that. She turned the laptop back toward herself and glanced at Kelly. "You do know he's an undercover cop, right? He practically reeks of it."

No, I don't! He bristled. *Look, kid, I've been fooling criminals into believing I was one of them since before you were alive.*

Kelly didn't answer. Instead, her gaze just ping-ponged back and forth between them and she had an inscrutable look on her face. The baby began to fuss. Kelly rocked the car seat gently and the baby stopped.

"And if your husband had stepped up

and been there for you last year," Liam said sharply, "instead of disappearing into the ether with his decipher key, or told the truth about how he'd hacked the code, then maybe none of this would've happened."

Any worry he'd pushed the young woman too far evaporated as he saw the fire flash in her dark eyes.

"My husband did what he did to protect me," Hannah said. "If he'd come forward after that bombing, my daughter and I probably wouldn't even be alive right now."

She couldn't possibly know that. But something pinged loudly before he could answer. She spun the laptop toward him.

"And apparently you're not above working with criminals," Hannah said. "You've got an incoming call from hacker Seth Miles."

Liam had no idea how Seth had breached the Imposters's cyberbubble and located Hannah's laptop. But he'd long stopped being surprised by what Seth could do.

"He's reformed," Liam said. He crossed the floor in three strides and Hannah moved out of the way to let him take her place behind the desk. He glanced at the screen. Seth's surprised face looked up at him.

"Seth, you're a genius," Liam said.

"I know," Seth said. The hacker looked every bit as confused as Liam had been feeling. The two women seemed to be fussing over the baby. Liam dropped into a chair and rolled it into the far corner of the room holding the laptop in one hand. "So you found Hannah Phillips?"

"Yup." Though she wasn't anything like what he'd expected and he still hadn't gotten to the bottom of Kelly's connection to all of this. "What's new?"

"No casualties or major injuries that we know of," Seth said. "Law enforcement's still trying to figure out who's even negotiating for the Imposters. What I want to know is how you managed to call me on a dark-web channel when I thought all connections in and out of the boat were down."

Liam froze.

Seth hadn't called Liam on Hannah's computer?

Hannah had called him?

A gust of cold air swept in to his right. Liam leaped to his feet. But it was too late. The women were gone. No, this wasn't happening. He hadn't been played. Not by such a basic distraction. He yanked back the door, but it caught after an inch. Seemed one of them had tied it shut with a baby blanket. His late father's tactical tip that everything was a potential weapon flickered unhelpfully in his mind. Dad had also been big on strategic distractions. Was Kelly going to use everything he'd taught her against him? He gritted his teeth and pulled harder. He could hear Seth's voice yelling behind him.

"Call you back!" Liam shouted. The fabric ripped and the door flew open. He ran out onto the deck and saw them. Hannah had climbed over the ledge and was lowering herself down by a ladder into a small speedboat below, which he guessed was one of the boats the Imposters had used to board the cruise ship. Kelly stood at the top of the ladder with the diaper bag over one shoulder and the car seat over the other.

Liam yanked his gun from its holster.

"Kelly!" he shouted as he ran to her side. "Step away from the ladder."

Kelly turned. He looked over the ledge. Hannah had reached the boat and her weapon was pointed right at him. He raised the weapon toward her. "Please, don't make me shoot you!"

"Liam! Stop!" Kelly shouted. She dropped the diaper bag and threw her arm between him and the boat. "Hannah is your daughter!"

My daughter?

His head swam, and he suddenly felt worse than he'd felt with any concussion he'd ever had. He had a daughter? Hannah Phillips was his daughter? The baby Kelly held was his granddaughter?

"She's your daughter," Kelly said again. "Our daughter. Our girl. I was pregnant when you dropped me off. I wrote and told you. I thought you knew. I always thought you knew."

He turned to her. His mouth opened but no words came out.

"Please, Liam." Pleading filled her gorgeous green eyes. "Come with us. Meet Renner and talk to him yourself. Consider it an undercover mission to meet a source. I don't care. Just, please, get on this boat and we can all leave together."

His heart stopped beating.

Help me, Lord. Please. Tell me what to do.

Gunfire sounded beneath them, mingled with the sound of Hannah screaming. He looked down to see two masked men, who it seemed had been hiding in the boat to ambush her, now holding Hannah at gunpoint.

"It's not Renner's boat!" Hannah cried in a panic. "They're Imposters!"

FOUR

Liam didn't have time to think. Maybe if he had, everything would've gone differently. But as the speedboat motor roared, he knew that within seconds Hannah would be kidnapped. Taken. Gone. And sometimes a person only got one chance do the right thing.

He leaped, launching himself overboard, then yanked out his weapon and fired on the way down. A bullet struck the controls. So far the goal was to stop them, nothing more. A man on the boat returned fire. Liam hit the boat and landed on the balls of his feet, just in time to note one of the Imposters throwing a fist toward his head. He blocked the blow and knocked the man back with one of his own.

The motorboat gunned beneath him, throwing him off balance.

"Don't move!" The man at the helm yanked Hannah against his chest and pressed a gun against her head. "Down on your knees, now! Or I'm shooting her!"

Liam paused a moment and prayed, as he analyzed the situation before him like an athlete would choreograph an upcoming play. First, he'd take out the man who was trying to punch him. Then, he'd turn the man's weapon on the criminal at the helm who was holding Hannah. Then, he'd turn the speedboat around.

But as he ran the plan through his head, the sound of angry shouting floated over the waters from the cruise ship behind him. Then he heard a plaintive and terrified sound fill the air. The baby was crying. He glanced back. The Imposters had captured Kelly.

"Save them!" Hannah begged, her voice rising above the noise of the boat's motor and the voices shouting. He turned to her.

Panic flooded her face. "Please, Liam! If you're really who my mother says you are, go rescue my mother and daughter! Please!"

And leave her to be kidnapped?

But before he could move, he heard a gunshot crack from the boat behind him and felt a bullet smack against the small of his back, wedging itself in his bulletproof vest and knocking him off balance. The engine gunned. He stumbled and fell, pitching against the side of the tiny boat as it swerved hard to the right. Then he fell overboard and into the dark waters below. Instantly the freezing water yanked him under, knocking his breath from his lungs. *Help me, God!* Inky blackness surrounded him on all sides. His gun had fallen from his grasp and he was sinking fast. He gritted his teeth and shed his jacket and sweater, then freed himself from the weight of his bulletproof vest, letting it sink down into the waters beneath him. Then he grabbed his jacket in one hand and forced his body to swim, the cold numbness in his limbs battling the burning pain in his lungs. He broke through the surface and gasped a breath. Chaos reigned around him.

The tiny speedboat was gone, taking Hannah with it and leaving nothing but the faint sound of a motor in its wake. On the cruise ship, masked Imposters surrounded Kelly. The lights of distant helicopters and rescue boats still hovered on the horizon, no doubt waiting for the signal from whoever was heading up the operation to board, and that person was probably waiting for some assurance of being able to keep the hostages safe. And somehow, through it all, one sound seemed to rise above it all. The tiny baby was crying out in fear.

And I will save her, so help me, God.

Still clenching his jacket in his freezing fingers, he swam, his aching body cutting through the dark waters toward the anchored boat. Thankfully, whoever had fired at him from the boat had stopped. He reached the rope ladder, forced his arms back through the sleeves of his sopping leather jacket and then began to climb, rung after rung, until he reached the top. Then he heard Kelly gasp his name. He surveyed the scene, his numb fingers still clutching the ladder's rungs. Four Imposter pirates greeted him. One with a yellow eye patch had his weapon pointed at Kelly. Green-and blue-eye-patched ones pointed their weapons at him. A red-eye-patched one held a camera phone. Looked like the new Imposters were filming the hijacking from multiple locations.

Out of all the bad options he had, his gut and his experience said the least bad one was to let himself get taken hostage. That way he could get back inside, warm up, dry off and catch his breath, and most importantly not start a firefight around a baby. Yet, as his eyes glanced at Kelly's face, he knew if she hadn't been there in the line of fire, and holding a child—*my grandchild*—that even battered, bruised and freezing numb, he'd have fought back, relying on the fact he knew how to fire, evade and disarm weapons like these better than these complete amateurs did.

He might've even won.

Instead, he slid his body over the edge. His knees hit the deck and stayed there, as the man in the green eye patch pressed his weapon against Liam's forehead.

"I'm detective Liam Bearsmith, RCMP," he said, "and I'm surrendering."

Kelly clutched the handle of Pip's car seat and she watched as Liam kneeled on the cruise boat's deck in the darkness with the barrel of a gun between his eyes. Maybe it was the cold, the darkness or the fact he was shivering, but the lines of his rugged jawline seemed even deeper than they had before. He'd gotten older, just like she had, and was no longer the seemingly indestructible young man he once was. And for the first time since he'd accosted her back on shore, she had the overwhelming urge to just throw her arms around him and keep him safe.

And maybe, if it hadn't been for little Pip, she would've.

Instead, she held her breath and prayed, for the baby beside her, the man at her feet and the daughter now being abducted by people willing to hurt her to get their hands on something that didn't even exist.

Help me, Lord. Tell me what to say. Show me what to do. Liam wasn't fighting back—he was surrendering. And somehow she knew it was because he wanted to keep her and Pip safe. *Is it my fault he's in danger?*

Maybe. Either way, she didn't just have to save Liam, she also had to get herself and the baby out of there. The Imposters were discussing what to do with Liam, debating whether or not to kill him. Apparently getting revenge on Liam's team for taking out the original Imposters was big on their to-do list. But that didn't mean they were in agreement about how to go about it. At least two of them thought they should just shoot Liam on the spot.

Despite slight variations in height and weight, there was something ubiquitous about them. As if these Imposters weren't individuals, but were just parts of an anonymous swarm. Maybe the anonymity emboldened them. Maybe it made this bunch of insecure, angry and violent young men feel important. The thought of begging, pleading and even bargaining with her own life to save Liam's crossed her mind. But two of Liam's tactical tips appeared in her memory as if with one voice. The first: know the enemy's weakness and use it against them. And the second: when facing the barrel of a gun, do whatever it takes to buy time.

"Are you a bunch of total amateurs?" she snapped, straightening to her full height like a mother scolding a group of rowdy teens. "You don't want to shoot him here! First of all, you're all about publicity and the lighting is terrible. Nobody will be able to see anything. Secondly, nobody will be able to hear anything properly with a baby crying. At least let me take the baby inside. Unless you want to sabotage your image by having every internet chat board discussing whether or not you're monsters for terrorizing a baby! Is that really the publicity you want?"

An odd strangled noise slipped from Liam's throat.

All four masked men turned to face her. She glanced past them to the rescue vehicles on the horizon, silently urging them to hurry up. Then she glanced back at the masked men.

"Thirdly, you guys are all in this for the attention, right?" she said. Her chin rose. "Well, you've got Canada's most significant, prolific and successful RCMP officer in your grasp, and you're debating whether or not to shoot him right here, right now? What's that going to accomplish? At least use him as a bargaining chip to get those helicopters and rescue boats out there to give you what you want. So get him back inside. Somewhere lit, where he can warm up and dry off enough to look threatening. Because right now he looks like a poor and feeble old man. With how bad the video will be out here, nobody will ever believe you four actually managed to capture the one and only Detective Liam Bearsmith."

A ripple seemed to move through the men as if each was imagining how it would look if they got the credit for ending Liam's life.

Then the man with the green eye patch ordered Liam to stand. Blue eye patch took Liam's cell phone, wallet and phone. Yellow eye patch hesitated for a moment, as if wondering what to do, and then took Kelly's diaper bag. The one with the red eye patch told them to move. They walked single file back inside the boat, with two men leading the way and two taking up the rear. Pip's cries fell silent, probably from a combination of movement and warmth. Kelly could feel Liam, just one step behind her. His hand brushed hers for a nanosecond, filling her with reassurance and strength. They walked down a hallway, climbed stairs, went down another hallway to another flight of stairs and then reached the third-level ballroom again. A man in a purple eye patch escorted them inside.

A couple hundred people sat on the floor in the large room, huddled together in clumps and talking to each other in whispers, while armed and masked men guarded them. She couldn't help but notice several passengers were recording video on their cell phones, although presumably none of them were online.

"Sit," the man with the red eye patch barked in her ear, so she did.

"I'll need my diaper bag back," she said, fixing her eyes on the man in the yellow eye patch and realizing he no longer had it. "So wherever you dropped it you'd better go get it."

His whole body flinched, as if he wasn't expecting a hostage to talk to him that way. He slipped out the door, as another one of the Imposters practically shoved Liam to sit.

For a moment Liam didn't even budge. Then he slowly sat down beside her. Liam waited until the guards moved back, then he leaned in and whispered, "Poor and feeble old man? Really?"

"Well, it worked, didn't it?" she whispered back.

He didn't answer and instead scanned the room. "Approximately a hundred and ninety hostages, give or take, and only four guards. Which puts them at a definite numbers disadvantage if it wasn't for how many rounds one of those weapons can get off in a minute."

"How's your back?" she asked. "Looked like you took a direct hit."

"Fine," he said. "Bit bruised but vest absorbed most of the impact. I've seen worse."

Somehow she suspected "I've seen worse" was his answer to a lot of things.

He glanced at her sideways. "Exactly what were you trying to accomplish with that speech?"

Seemed he wasn't about to let that go. "I was trying to buy you time, get us inside and use their obvious weaknesses against them."

"I had the situation under control."

Had he now? She felt her eyes roll and turned away to hide it. The baby cried softly. Not a full-out wail, just the kind of whimpering that meant she was looking for attention. Kelly rocked the car seat gently and prayed that rescue was imminent. Then she leaned down, brushed her lips over the soft top of the baby's head and prayed.

"To be honest, my biggest worry was something happening to you and the baby," he said. "When you've faced down as many evil amateurs with weapons as I have, you get a fairly good sense of how to get out of a situation like that with the minimum number of bullet holes. Turns out it's a whole different situation when you've got someone else to worry about." His hand reached out as if wanting to brush Pip's face and then stopped, like he was worried of accidentally breaking her. "Sorry, you never told me her name."

"We call her Pip."

"Seriously?" He quirked an eyebrow. "Pip Phillips?"

"It's a nickname," Kelly explained. "Renner's family tradition is you don't name a baby until both her parents have held her and Renner hasn't seen her yet. In Alberta, they have a year to register her name before it becomes a problem."

Liam nodded slowly and for a long moment he didn't say anything.

"I'm sorry I couldn't save Hannah," he said softly. "But we'll find her. I promise." Then his dark and soulful eyes turned back to her face. "So Hannah's our daughter?"

He whispered the last word so quietly it almost moved silently over his lips.

"Yeah." She nodded and something in his gaze was so intense she couldn't hold it any longer and instead looked down at the baby. "And this is really your granddaughter."

She looked around at the room again with its huddled groups of whispering and terrified people intent on recording every moment until their phone batteries died, even though their internet had been cut off. The jittery guards seemed to be growing more agitated and nervous by the second. "Although this really isn't how I wanted to tell you."

"Okay," Liam said softly.

It was amazing how a single word could carry so much weight.

"How old was Hannah when you, when they…" His words trailed off.

"When she was adopted?" Kelly asked. "A couple of hours. Her parents were there in the delivery room. They let me hold her. They were really good people. I owe them everything. They died a few years ago. Hannah found me then."

And Kelly had known, somehow, that it was right to entrust them with Hannah, let them raise her and be her parents. She'd known then and never doubted it was right. Even though giving them her baby girl had felt like tearing off a piece of her own heart.

"You never had kids?" she asked.

"I've got no family." He shook his head and chuckled softly, as if the sound was coming from somewhere very deep inside him. "I've never even kissed anyone who wasn't you."

A door slammed open behind her. She glanced back to see the man with the yellow eye patch stride through, her diaper bag under his arm.

"You!" He pointed at her with the butt of his gun. "Lady with the baby. Stand up. You're coming with me."

FIVE

But as Kelly got to her feet, she felt Liam's hand grab hold of hers.

"I'm going with her!" Liam's voice rose and seemed to boom around the room. "They're not going anywhere without me."

As if on cue, the masked men focused their weapons on Liam, filling the air with shouts, swearing and threats. Pip's cries grew into a full-throated wail. She needed to get the baby out of there. Unless the Imposters had thoroughly searched the diaper bag and found each hidden compartment, there might still be an encrypted burner phone and mini–stun gun inside it, along with other helpful tools. She couldn't miss her opportunity to get her hands on them.

"Please, lady," the man in the yellow eye patch said. "You've got to come with me. Now."

There was a slight waver in his voice, almost like he was pleading with her. Did Liam hear it, too? Or was he too focused on the cacophony around them? She didn't know. But another of his tactics filled her mind. *Nobody's fully evil.* Every enemy has the potential to do the right thing. Was the man in the yellow eye patch trying to do the right thing now?

"It's okay," she said, glancing at Liam. "I've got to get Pip out of here and to somewhere quieter. We'll be okay. And if not, you'll find us."

His jaw set, and something hardened like flint behind his eyes. "You're sure right I will."

She swallowed hard and the man with the yellow eye patch practically pushed the diaper bag into her hand. She prayed that everything she needed was still inside. The Imposter led her out of the room and down a hallway, until they reached a door in the wall. He opened it and she looked inside. It seemed to be a cross between a security office and a supply room. A clunky monitor in the corner flickered black-and-white security camera footage of the chaos she'd left behind in the ballroom, but the rest of the space was crammed tightly with spare linens, decorations and chairs for the events. But, thankfully, it had a table she could change Pip on.

"I'm not a bad person," the anonymous man with the yellow eye patch said. "Just so you know. I just believe the wrong people are running the world, the system is rigged against the little guy and someone needs to teach them a lesson."

So had how many other people across the world throughout history? The mother's heart inside her found itself praying for him. And that he'd live long enough to both repent and grow.

She took the diaper bag from his hand

and walked into the room, planning out her next steps as she did so. She would set down Pip, pretend to search the bag for a diaper and then get the mini–stun gun. She'd get close enough to zap him, then tie him up with some of the brightly colored decorative cord on the shelf. And then, what? *Help me, Lord.*

"I'll just be one moment," she said. She took the diaper bag from him and put it on the table, wishing she didn't have to turn her back on him even if it was only for a moment.

"Stay here," he said. "You'll be safe if you stay in here."

The door slammed shut. Something clicked.

"Wait!" She turned quickly. "Stop!"

She set down Pip, crossed the floor and grabbed the handle. It turned but the door didn't budge. Instead, as she pulled she just heard the thump of metal against the frame. Her heart leaped into her throat.

For a second it pounded so hard she could barely breathe. They were locked in.

Pip's cries rose again. Kelly ran back to her, unclipped her from the car seat and held her to her chest. "Shh. It's okay. Don't worry. It's all going to be okay."

She rocked back and forth, shifting her weight from one foot to the other. Her gaze ran to the security camera, trying to seek out Liam's form on the small screen. But whether it was the angle, the crowd or something else that had happened to him, she couldn't see him anywhere.

Lord, keep him safe. Keep Hannah safe. Keep Pip and I safe. We all need You now.

Liam was right. It was different when there was somebody else to care for. When she and Liam had been on the run when they were younger, it had just been a matter of fight, run, hide and survive. But how could she do that with a baby? Somehow the true weight of being a mother hadn't really hit her until the moment Hannah had told her she'd be taking the

Ugly Sweater Holiday Cruise as a cover to escape Canada and rejoin Renner. And now the weight of her love for Hannah and Pip seemed heavy enough to crush her heart.

"You see, Pip," she told the tiny baby, as she rocked her back and forth, "the thing with being a mom is sometimes you've got to let your children make their own decisions. Your mommy loves your daddy so much, was so determined to be with him and so convinced he was right, that my choices were either to rat them out to law enforcement, let her go on her own or agree to go with her, to take care of you and try to keep her safe. She said once we met up with your daddy, he'd explain everything and I would understand. But now we're locked in a closet on a hijacked boat. And I've gotta figure out how to get out of here while keeping you safe."

The baby's cries stopped. She waltzed Pip over to the table, opened the diaper bag, put down a change mat and laid Pip on top of it. Pip looked at her, with wide eyes, and kicked and waved her limbs.

"Now, listen to me," Kelly said as she emptied the bag onto the table. "You and I are not going to fall apart. We're made of tougher stuff than that, little Pip. You and I are going to hold it together, and figure our way out of this one step at a time."

Her fingers brushed a pacifier. It was pink and had a duck on it. She popped it into Pip's mouth. The baby sucked on it thoughtfully. Kelly kept searching. *Thank You, God!* The mini–stun gun was still there, along with a backup roll of both Canadian and American cash, an old-fashioned compass and the encrypted cell phone. No handgun or computer, though. She turned on the phone. It had a little bit of battery left but no cell signal. No phone charger, either. She let out a long breath.

"Well, it's literally a mixed bag," she told Pip. "But the good news is we've got enough formula to last twenty-four hours. It might be lukewarm and we're just going to have to make do with that. One way or another, we're getting out of this. Your grandfather's a really good guy and the strongest man I've ever met. If anyone can find us, it's him. And if not, we'll find our way out of here and go find him."

A lump caught in her throat. She ignored it. Pip needed her to be strong right now and that's what she was going to do. That and pray.

Sudden movement on the monitor drew her eyes back. Seemed the Imposters had ordered everyone to their feet. She watched as the hostages stood, quaking and holding their hands in the air, some still clutching their phones. What was this? What was happening? Then through the crowd, she saw Liam. His eyes were locked on the camera, defiant and unflinching.

A faint haze moved across the top of the screen, like a distortion or smoke moving across the top of the room. Liam's nose twitched and his gaze rose as if sensing something.

Then as she watched, people began to fall, collapsing and dropping to the ground like marionettes whose strings had just been cut.

Liam held his breath. Whatever it was they were piping in through the air vents, it felt thick, smelled sickly sweet and had the people around him dropping like flies. No doubt it looked pretty impressive on camera. But was it deadly? Hopefully not. Screams rose around him. People were panicking, collapsing and fainting. For a moment, he couldn't even see their Imposter captors in the mayhem. He quickly crouched beside an elderly woman to his right and checked her pulse. Seemed like she'd fainted.

Whatever the toxin or illness, the very old and very young were invariably the most at risk. He prayed hard that Kelly and the baby were okay. But first, he had to take care of the hostages. *Help me, God.* He yanked the neckline of his shirt up over his nose and mouth and focused on moderating his breathing to inhale as little toxin as possible.

He fought the urge to raise his voice and shout at everyone to stay calm. He'd need every breath right now.

Every gas he knew that knocked a person out tended to take a different amount of time for different people, depending on all sorts of factors, from age, to build, to even how much they'd eaten. Thanks to his build, metabolism and his ability to moderate his breathing, he'd probably be the last man standing. But it was only a matter of time before he, too, fell.

He scanned the room, pushing his way through the panic. Then his eyes locked on the Imposters. Three remained, standing between him and the doors leading out to the fresh air on deck. All of them looked wobbly and unsteady, even like they were shaking.

Huh. Guess none of their friends warned them about the gas. But that matched what he knew about the criminals. Seemed it really was every Imposter for himself.

So three woozy, probably panicked and confused gun-wielding men stood between him and breathable air. Liam didn't even hesitate. He charged, lowering his head, and plowed his body right into the chest of the nearest man, praying he'd catch him off guard before he had the chance to try and pull the trigger. Bull's-eye. He caught him in a football tackle and planted his shoulder into the man's sternum while one hand wrenched the weapon from his grasp. The Imposter went sprawling. Liam glanced at the gun and almost growled. It wasn't even loaded. Again, not surprising considering an ad hoc online mob would likely have some problems arming themselves.

Hopefully, the other two masked men's weapons were equally ineffective. Either way, it was a risk he was about to take.

"Drop your weapons!" Liam bellowed, swinging the useless weapon around and aiming it at the two Imposters on the other side of the room. "Now!"

They dropped their weapons so quickly it was like their arms had collapsed. Good. *Thank You, God.* One problem down. A bunch more to go.

His experienced eyes quickly scanned the room, looking for anyone in the chaos who still potentially had their head on straight.

"You!" He gestured first to an athletic-looking middle-aged couple near the middle of the room and then to two fit young women in matching sweaters at the far end. "Secure those weapons. Throw them overboard if you need to. Just don't let anyone else get a hold of them."

People throwing semiautomatic weapons overboard would be as good a sign as any to those law-enforcement people in hovering helicopters and rescue boats that it was time to swoop in and make their move despite whatever story the designated Imposter hostage negotiator they were talking to was feeding them.

"All right, everyone!" His voice rose above the chaos. "If you can crawl, get outside. If you can walk, drag someone who can't with you."

"The doors are locked!" a woman shouted.

Yeah, but not for long.

"Everybody get back!" Liam grabbed one of the tall tables with his free hand, swung it around like a club and smashed it through the window. Glass shattered and cold, clean, pure night air rushed in. Liam dove through the window, hit the deck and rolled to his feet. Sure enough, someone had looped what looked like bicycle locks around the door handles. Cheap and effective, and he was about to break them off. The table he'd bashed through the window had seen better days, but all it took him was one of the legs to break through the lock and tear the door handle off. The door flew open and people rushed through.

He quickly glanced at the rescue helicopters circling in the sky and waved both hands above his head. He'd been behind the scenes of enough hostage situations to know not to judge when rescuers made their move. It was possible the Imposters were feeding them all sorts of nonsense and stringing them on with all kinds of false threats and negotiation points. And he had no idea what signal they were waiting for that it was go-time.

Well, he was now giving them a pretty big one.

He glanced both ways down the deck and didn't see a single Imposter. He wasn't sure if that meant they'd run or just pulled off their masks and mingled with the crowd. He ran down the deck to the next door and the next lock. This one was heavy-duty, so this time he wedged his piece of broken table leg into the door frame and, with the help of a couple of partygoers, bent it back until the door broke free of its hinges. More people poured past him. Some led or carried loved ones and strangers along with them. Others pushed and shoved as they stampeded for the door. And his job was to save them all. One whiff of the air that accompanied them and he could tell the toxin was growing thicker. The dizziness in his head warned him if he inhaled any more, he was at risk of passing out.

He ran back in, feeling his body being buffeted by those streaming out. He prayed with every breath that Kelly and Pip had fresh air to breathe. Either way, he'd give his final breath for them. The room was emptying fast. He ran across the polished floor toward the door that the man with the yellow eye patch had led Kelly and the baby through. Then he saw another young woman passed out on the floor. She was waif thin and barely four feet, but, thankfully, she was breathing. He dropped his piece of broken table and bulletless gun, scooped her up into his arms and ran back toward the deck. He spotted a broad-shouldered man, at least six foot seven, Liam guessed, helping a couple of other men get the last few remaining partygoers out the door.

"Officer!" Liam shouted. It was an educated guess given the young man's bearing and one that proved correct when he turned. Liam locked eyes with him. "You—I need you to come and take her."

Without missing a beat, the young man did a swift check of those around him, made sure they were okay without his help and then jogged toward Liam.

"Up-to-date on CPR accreditation?" Liam asked. The man nodded, looking baffled. Liam eased the tiny woman into the man's arms. Her eyes fluttered and Liam was thankful she was conscious. "Police division?"

"I'm from York Region," he replied. "But I haven't passed the academy yet. I'm not actually a cop."

Not yet, but he would be.

"I'm Detective Liam Bearsmith, RCMP," he said. "Come find me when you graduate."

He allowed himself one more gasp of fresh air, then he ran back through the ballroom. It was empty now, but he still yanked back tablecloths and looked underneath to make sure no one was left. The air seemed to thicken around him. He pushed his body deeper and deeper into the sickly sweet and pungent smoke. The walls and floor undulated around him, as if he was underwater. Somehow he'd lost sight of where he'd dropped the bulletless gun and his makeshift weapon, but thankfully another broken table leg wasn't hard to find. Or was it the same one? He couldn't tell. He leaned on it like a crutch and pushed through, inhaling more and more knockout gas into his lungs with every breath. He had to find her. He had to make sure she was safe, even as he could feel the heaviness of the toxin filling his body like quicksand dragging him down.

He reached a door, yanked the handle and found it locked. He swung back with the broken table leg, then smashed the handle over and over again until the door broke free of the frame. He fell through it, back into the same kitchen he'd been in before, and immediately the air felt lighter. He stumbled through, thankful to see the door to the pantry where he'd once found hostages was now open and the room was empty. Hopefully they'd made it to where the air was clean.

As for him, he now stayed upright by sheer willpower alone.

"Kelly!" He stumbled down the hall, forcing her name through his burning lungs, yanking open doors and almost tumbling through, as the ship seemed to move like it was being tossed in an ever-worsening storm.

Then he saw a bicycle lock looped around a doorknob ahead and on his right.

He blinked, as his vision focused on the black-and-gold object sitting on the floor, propped up against the frame as if someone had left it there waiting just for him. He bent down and reached for it, stumbling and falling against the door. No, it couldn't be, he had to be hallucinating. His fingers clamped on to the object, feeling its old, familiar form.

It was his police badge.

But who had left it there? And why?

"Liam?" The sound of Kelly's voice calling his name cut through his foggy brain. The door shook in front of him as if someone was trying to jar it loose from the frame.

"Kelly..." He forced her name over his heavy tongue.

"Liam!" Her voice rose, full of strength and joy. "We're in here! Pip and I are okay. But the door is locked!" *Not for long.* "Is everything okay? There's a monitor in here. I saw people fainting and you helping break them out."

"The Imposters pumped some kind of knockout gas into the air vents," he said. "Big snazzy finale. But now law enforcement will move in and secure the boat." In moments it would all be over. Liam would make sure Kelly and Pip were taken to a safe house, where someone he trusted would watch over them. And he could talk to his team and figure out how they were going to find Hannah. "Step back and take cover. I'm going to break the door down. Not much gas in the air out here, but you'll want to inhale as little as possible and help shield the baby until we're outside."

The lock was lighter than the other ones, flimsy even, but his swings felt slower, heavier and sluggish. The door fell open and there stood Kelly.

His heart caught in his throat.

Had she always been this beautiful? Dark hair fell around her face in waves. Her green eyes sparkled with a warmth that made him think of happiness and home. Her gorgeous lips parted slightly in the smile that had never once, in over twenty years, left the edges of his heart.

"Liam!" Her voice was sharp, almost worried. Her hand brushed his face. "Are you okay? You look dazed."

He was fine. He was just sleepy, his head was woozy and things weren't quite looking right.

She slung the diaper bag determinedly over her shoulder and picked up the car seat. There was a small baby in a pink knit hat inside.

Oh, right... Pip. I—I have a grand-daughter.

Kelly's other hand grabbed his and squeezed it so tightly he almost winced.

"Come on," she said. "We're getting you out of here before you pass out."

She ran down the hallway, carrying the baby's car seat in one hand and pulling him after her with the other. Stairs seemed to rise and fall beneath him as he stumbled down them like he was in a fun house. They pushed through a door and stepped out onto the deck. Cold winter night air filled his lungs. Noise and lights assailed his senses. Law enforcement had arrived, and the boat was being evacuated.

"This way." Kelly grabbed his arm and pulled him down the deck, away from the rescue operations. "We have to try and get Hannah's laptop. I'm sure she wiped it clean but maybe we can find a way to use it to track her. I just hope it's still there."

"Stop!" a voice barked. Liam turned to see a young man in a black-blue Toronto police uniform. "Police! Drop your weapon!"

What? What weapon?

It was only then Liam realized he was still clutching the piece of broken table leg he'd used to break open the doors. He let it fall to the deck with a clatter, yanked his badge and held it up.

"De Tec'ive Leeyam Bears-s-smith," he called, his words slurring. "Rrrr. Cee. Em'p."

The cop swore at him. "Get down!" he barked. "Now!"

Who was the cop talking to? Liam turned and looked behind him, feeling the world spin out of focus. There was no one there.

"Duuuuude," Liam shouted. "Chilllll!"

But it was like the cop didn't even hear him.

"Ma'am!" he shouted. "Step away from the suspect."

What suspect? What was going on?

"Get down!" The cop's voice rose. "Now!"

Liam didn't understand. None of this was making sense. "Look, kid, I'm detective Liam Bearsmith..."

His words felt thick and mushy on his tongue.

"Stop lying!" the cop shouted. "You keep that name out of your filthy mouth. You hear me? You don't get to lie about something like that. It's disrespecting the uniform and everyone who wears it." The cop was definitely getting heated.

"Hey, buddy," Liam said, as firmly as he could muster. "Cool it."

"You get down and stop talking," the cop said. "Now, or I'll shoot!"

Shoot him? For what? For saying his own name? For holding his badge?

Was this really happening? Was he hallucinating all this?

The cop rushed toward him with his weapon raised. Liam's knees began to buckle beneath him. Then he felt Kelly pull away from his grasp. Liam stumbled. His knees hit the deck.

"I'm arresting you on suspicion of murder and impersonating a police officer—"

He felt a hand on the back of his head shoving him against the deck. His hands were wrenched behind his back. Pain shot through his injured back. A handcuff clicked over his right wrist. The cop struggled to secure the second.

Help me, Lord! What's happening to me?

Something crackled loudly by his face and flashed like bright blue lightning.

Something thudded to the deck beside him. A hand grabbed his and pulled him up.

"Come on!" Kelly's voice swam somewhere around the edges of his mind. "You can still run, right?"

He didn't know if he could. He didn't know if he could even walk, or how long he'd be able to outrun the unconsciousness threatening to pull him under. He'd inhaled so much gas that he should be out cold by now. His feet stumbled beneath him, and he was barely able to complete each step he took. Lights and noise seemed to screech at the corners of his barely conscious mind. Then it was like the sky above him was exploding in a bright, wild and inexplicable array of popping sounds and dazzling color. Fireworks? How? He felt something bash into his stomach so hard it winded him. He pitched forward.

And the last thing Liam Bearsmith knew was that he was falling.

SIX

Air rushed past him. He was tumbling and falling into darkness. Something cold and hard smacked against his body. Pain shot through him. Unconsciousness swept over him. He tried to fight it, willing himself to move, only to feel his body collapse beneath him. Then he felt the vibrations of an engine seemingly rumbling around him and heard Kelly's reassuring voice promising him that everything was going to be okay. Something warm fell over his body. And then there was nothing but sleep.

He had no idea how long he'd been out when he felt something jolt him back to consciousness. He opened his eyes. The sky was still dark, but now the world had fallen silent. He was lying on the floor of a small motorboat. Stars peeked through the moving clouds above. Water lapped gently against ice. A blanket was over his body, and what looked like an empty water bottle and empty bag of animal crackers were on the floor by his face.

A light flickered on ahead of him, shining over his face.

He sat up, his hands shielding his face from the light, and he felt the weight of a handcuff dangling from one wrist.

"I'm—"

"Detective Liam Bearsmith," Kelly said. "I know. You say that a lot. But this is one problem just shouting your name won't solve."

Oh, ha ha. The light moved from his face down to his feet. He was sitting in the back of a small speedboat that was docked at what looked like a tiny island no bigger than the size of one of those large backyards in the suburbs. Kelly was standing on the shore. A small cabin, not much more than a shack, sat behind her. Dim light flickered in a window.

"Welcome back," she said. "You finally going to stay awake on me this time?"

Yeah, he had the vague sense he'd woken up before, but couldn't really remember it.

"Where's Pip?" he asked.

"Safe in the cabin." She swung her light to the building only a few feet behind her. "I built a little nest out of blankets and pillows for her on the floor. She's excited to wriggle and move. But she'll start crying for me if I'm gone more than two minutes. No electricity, but there is well water coming out of the tap. I was able to light a lamp and there's a gas heater I can use to heat Pip's bottle. She was getting tired of drinking it cold."

"You broke into a cottage?" he asked.

"The key was on a hook under a welcome sign beside the front door," she said. "It wasn't exactly hidden."

And that wasn't exactly a denial.

"How did we get here?" he asked. "How did we even get off the boat?"

"Renner's original plan was to dock a small and undetectable motorboat off the port side of the cruise ship," she said. "Hannah and I were supposed to wait for a big distraction and take off during the confusion. I was steering you, trying to find Renner's boat, when a whole lot of fireworks went off at once. It was utter chaos. You fell and landed in the boat. We took off. Sure enough, the fireworks and general mayhem provided enough distraction for us to escape without being caught. No one was chasing after one tiny speedboat in all that. Plus, I kept the lights completely off until we cleared Lake Ontario, so we'd have been pretty hard to spot, especially when people had their hands full of a boat full of Imposters and rescued hostages."

He frowned.

"That whole explanation is ridiculous," he said. "If Renner set up fireworks to help Hannah escape wouldn't they have gone off earlier? Wouldn't it make more sense for the Imposters to have set them off to make a giant spectacle or give them cover for escaping? And driving off in a speedboat like that with the lights off was risky. You had no way of knowing you'd evade detection."

She crossed her arms. "Well apparently it worked because we weren't captured and we're here now."

"Where are we anyway?" he asked.

"On one of the Thousand Islands in the St. Lawrence River," she said. She swung the light up a flagpole by the cottage to where an American flag hung limp. "We're on US soil," she added. "So you've got no jurisdiction to arrest me."

He snorted. The Thousand Islands were a stretch of small islands in the St. Lawrence River between Canada and the United States. Some had houses on them and others had cabins or cottages. Many were nothing more than a rock. There was often no way to tell which side of the border each one was on if it wasn't for the flags, and some even spanned the border.

It wasn't a half-bad place to hide. Not that she hadn't been completely wrong to run from the authorities.

"We've had this exact same conversation before," she added. "But you kept falling back asleep. We don't have a lot of gas left in the tank, Renner still hasn't responded to any of my messages and my phone is almost dead. This seemed like a good place to stop and regroup."

Maybe, but they shouldn't have to stop and regroup. She should be back in Toronto, fast asleep in a well-guarded safe house or hotel room, while he figured out this whole thing with the police.

"I only have a few minutes of battery left on my phone," she said, "but is there anyone you need to contact? Any family or friends who'll be worried about you or wonder why you didn't come home?"

"Told you, I have no family," Liam said.

There'd just been Dad and he'd died four years ago. "Or friends like that, really. What I need to do is contact my team and come up with a strategy to handle this."

She pressed her lips together. "Then let me talk to Renner first. The phone is very close to dying and I need to tell him what happened to Hannah. Then you can have it to call whoever you need."

"If the Imposters have Hannah they'll have posted about it on the dark web," Liam said. "Whether they'll be bragging about it or just putting out feelers trying to attract Renner's attention, either way, they definitely won't keep quiet about it. That means Seth will spot it, know what's happened immediately and alert my team. Law enforcement will already be looking for her. They won't hurt her, I'm sure of it. Based on my experience and what we've seen, they like chaos, not cruelty."

At least for now. It had only been a few hours, but who knew what would happen if the situation dragged on.

"You told me all that before, too," Kelly said, "and hearing it helped keep me sane. So, thank you. Also, we need to get online as soon as possible."

"I really don't think surfing the web is a priority," he said.

"Anything could have happened while we were off-line," she said. "The whole world could be different."

Not that different. She turned to go back to the cabin.

"We shouldn't even be here," he said. "Just because your plan apparently worked doesn't mean it wasn't completely wrong, risky and ridiculous. We shouldn't have left the boat. We should have gone with the police."

She stopped and turned back. Her hands snapped to her hips, sending the light to her feet. "One, we've already talked about this, every single time you've woken up, even if you keep forgetting. Two, I saved your life. And three, that police offer wanted to arrest you for murder."

Yeah, but that was the part that hadn't made any sense.

"Look, that was obviously a misunderstanding that would've been cleared up immediately," he said.

"And I think that you're wrong and I made the right call," she said. "But I don't really care if you believe me right now. I've got to get back to Pip and keep trying to reach Renner."

Before he could splutter another word, she turned and walked back to the cabin, taking the light with her. Frustration burned in the back of his throat. Who did this woman think she was? If she'd been anyone else, he might've actually thought she'd kidnapped him. That idea was almost enough to make him chuckle. But, no, this whole situation was not happening this way.

Lord, help me handle this mess the right way. And help her listen to me.

He glanced around the boat. Thankfully, he couldn't see any form of tracking device and the boat wasn't fancy enough for an onboard computer. So she was probably right no one had tracked them. The keys weren't in the ignition, but it would be easy enough to hot-wire if he needed to. He couldn't tell how low they were on gas. But the river was narrow enough that he could probably make it to shore on fumes. If need be, he could swim back to Canada.

He headed for the cottage, knocked twice on the door and then pushed it open. Warmth swept around him. Kelly looked up from where she sat cross-legged on a blanket on the floor. Pip was lying on her back, with her eyes seemingly locked on Kelly's face. She was waving all four limbs at once and making this cute little cooing sound Liam had never heard before. It was like Pip was trying to talk. A light filled Kelly's face as she looked down at the tiny child, and as frustrated as he was with her, something about it still took his breath away. When he'd been a much younger man he'd thought Kelly Marshall was the most attractive woman he'd ever seen. But now, two decades later, there was something so much deeper and richer to her beauty that defied description.

She looked up at him.

"I know it's not much," she said. "But I figured it was safer that we stop somewhere and get warm than just keep going in below-freezing temperatures until the gas ran out."

It was only then he looked away, long enough to look around. The cabin was one large room. There was a couch with a mattress wedged upright behind it, a small table with two chairs and a kitchen counter with a bucket sitting under the open pipe of the sink. A small array of candles of different sizes and shapes flickered from various surfaces. The gas heater was at least fifty years old and the small fire burning within it was warming a battered pot of water she'd placed on top of it.

"Don't worry," she said. "I'll lock the door before I leave and leave more than enough cash to cover what I used. I have a couple thousand dollars in emergency money in the diaper bag. Hannah and I emptied our bank accounts."

Defiance rumbled in her voice. The flames around them reflected in her eyes. He opened a drawer and rooted around until he found a paper clip. Then he picked the handcuff lock and took it off.

"You've gotten better at picking handcuffs," she said. "Used to take you a lot longer than that."

"I've gotten a lot of practice," he said. He noticed her phone was sitting beside her on the floor. "Have you heard from Renner?"

"No," she said.

Worry washed over her features, wiping the smile from her face. Should he feel guilty about that? She was the one who'd made wrong call after wrong call.

"We're not staying here," Liam said and sat down on the carpet opposite her.

"Do whatever you want," she said. "But I'm going to wait for a message from Renner and figure out how I'm going to find my daughter."

Considering the depth of pain and worry in her eyes, he decided not to read anything into the fact she'd said "my" instead of "ours."

"Look," Liam said, "as romantic as it might be to paint Hannah and Renner as just two foolish kids in love, who were trying to run off into the sunset together, law enforcement exists for a reason."

"Says the man who—"

"Who broke all the rules and was willing to throw his entire career away to be with you some twenty years ago?" Liam interrupted her, completing the sentence. "I know, foolish kids in love don't always make the best decisions, Kelly. Believe me, I get the irony."

Her mouth set in a thin line.

"Actually," she said, "I was going to say 'the man who is willing to have a criminal hacker like Seth Miles on his team.' I know Seth's reputation. I know what he's done. He broke the law, repeatedly, which is more than you can say for Renner or Hannah."

Yes, but Seth had turned his life around and had believed he was doing the right thing at the time when he'd hacked criminals and worked outside the law to bring down bad guys. But if Liam pointed that out, Kelly would only counter that Hannah and Renner thought they were doing the right thing, too. Liam had perused Seth's file enough to know that unlike Liam's father—who'd done his best in his own faulty way to protect him—Seth's high-ranking military father had been downright abusive, which had instilled in him a deep distrust of anything law enforcement. The steps Seth had made to help his team in the past year had been a series of huge steps of personal growth.

Seth's past choices weren't right, but they were forgivable.

Pip squealed loudly. Liam looked down. She seemed to be trying to figure out how to twist and turn her body around to face him.

"She wants you to pick her up," Kelly said.

He'd take her word for it. He didn't pick up the baby, but he did shift his body around the carpet so that she could look up at him. Pip smiled, and he found himself smiling back.

"Believe me," Kelly said, "I argued against Hannah and Renner's plan until I was blue in the face. But at the end of the day, my options were to let her go alone or agree to go with her. I figured at least if I went with her I could keep Pip safe and try to talk some sense into them. Despite what you might think, Renner and Hannah aren't criminals. Renner was working as a military contractor, decoded a terrorist's online code and stopped a major bombing—"

"And within hours the internet was reporting he'd done so by creating a master-key decryption device," Liam added. "One which by rights would've belonged to the Canadian government."

And which, to be fair, was one that a lot of terrorist groups were suddenly ready to kidnap and kill Renner's young family to get their hands on. Liam could give Renner that much.

"Yup," she agreed, "and then he nearly died in a targeted bomb strike. So he went underground until he could find a way to reunite safely with his secretly pregnant wife. Are you saying that's any different than what you would've done?"

Liam gritted his teeth. Maybe not, but he wasn't twenty-two anymore.

"It's not illegal to walk out of witness protection," Kelly said. "I get you had the right to detain Hannah for questioning. But how exactly is it a crime to steal a decryption key that doesn't exist? Or to aid and abet someone accused of stealing a nonexistent thing?"

"How did a low-level engineer in Afghanistan decode a code that complex without the assistance of a decryption key?" Liam asked, and he'd keep on asking until he got an answer.

"How does my witness-protection file say I married a man named Robbie, had four sons and died?" she challenged. "How did the Imposters track us to the boat?"

"Obviously they had a tail on you or Hannah," Liam said.

"Or they had a tail on you," she countered, "and it was a fluke they saw Hannah. Or maybe Seth is an Imposter."

"That's not possible." He could feel the scowl on his face. "We're wasting time and you're being just as foolish as Hannah and Renner. I need to call my team, get them to relocate you and Pip somewhere safe and ensure they're focusing the full might of law enforcement on finding Hannah."

"So you're just going to ignore the fact that a cop tried to arrest you for murder," she said. "He had one handcuff on you and a knee in your back before I rescued you."

The memory of the zapping sound and flash of light filled his mind. Zapping a police officer with a mini–stun gun and then running off with his suspect was most definitely a crime.

"I didn't want or need to be rescued," he said.

"He called you a liar," she said. "Look, I don't know who he thinks you killed. If only we could get online, we could figure that out. But he was really steamed up about it."

"He was just a bad cop!" Liam's voice rose. "There are a few bad cops out there. But a whole lot more who are good ones."

"My gut says he was looking for any excuse to shoot you for resisting arrest."

"Your gut is wrong."

Pip whimpered. He glanced down. The baby's chin was quivering.

"She can tell you're angry," Kelly said.

"I'm not angry," Liam said. He scooped up Pip onto his lap, turned her to face him and made himself smile. "See, Pip?" His voice rose an octave. "It's all good. Nothing to cry about. I'm not angry. I just think your grandma did something very silly."

Pip stopped crying but she didn't smile. Instead she looked at him skeptically, as if to say "yeah, sure." He hadn't known someone so tiny could call him out so thoroughly.

Kelly chuckled softly under her breath. And suddenly it hit him: she could've just taken off with the baby and left him behind to be arrested. Probably would've made her life a whole lot simpler.

"Look," he said, trying another tack. "I get that I was practically unconscious, that cop's behavior was bizarre, it probably seemed safer to make a quick escape and that considering the freezing temperatures, taking shelter indoors made sense." He bounced the baby and kept his voice upbeat and cheerful. Pip latched her tiny fingers around his. "But I fundamentally disagree with every call you've made."

And yet defiance still filled her eyes. She was just so convinced that she was right and he was wrong. In a world full of people, how was this woman the only one he'd ever thought himself in love with? Two of his teammates were getting married in the next forty-eight hours and a third was getting married on New Year's Eve. Somehow those couplings had always made sense. His gut told him that Mack the detective and Iris the social worker just belonged together, as did Detective Jess with former detective Travis and Detective Noah with Corporal Holly. So how was it the only woman for him had been someone this obstinate, difficult, challenging and impossible?

Kelly shrugged. "All I can do is tell you

what happened," she said. "If I made the wrong call, I'm sorry. But at least I made it trying to save your life."

She stretched her hand out toward him. For a moment his eyes lingered on her face, then he looked down at her hand. She was offering him her burner phone.

"It's secure," she said, "according to Hannah. But it's also down to less than five percent battery power. It could die at any moment. It was only supposed to be used to send encrypted messages to Renner. But he's not responding. You might not trust me, but I still trust you."

She placed the phone into his palm and their fingers brushed. Then she stood up, walked over to the small stove and pulled the pot of water off the heat. She put the pot in the sink and set a bottle of formula inside it to warm up.

Liam dialed Seth's number.

"Hello, you've reached Seth Miles..." The hacker's voice was oddly formal. Despite the fact it was the middle of the night, he'd answered on the first ring. "How can I help you?"

"Hey, it's me," he said. "It's Liam. Good news—I'm still alive. I can't tell you how thankful I am to hear your voice—"

"Sorry, sir," Seth interrupted quickly. "I think you got the wrong number."

Liam's eyes rolled. Did Seth think he was being funny?

"Seth, don't start with me," Liam said. "I've been through way too much in one night for jokes right now."

"And I'm saying, you dialed the wrong number," Seth said.

The phone went dead. Liam blinked. Seth had hung up on him.

He looked at Kelly. She'd barely let the bottle sit in the water a few moments and already she was tapping out a few drops of formula milk on the inside of her elbow. She frowned and set the bottle back in the water.

"Why did he just hang up on me?" he

asked. "What do I need to know about this number?"

"I don't know," she said. "All I know is it's encrypted. Should be impossible to trace. Of course, that doesn't mean someone isn't tracing Seth's phone from the other end."

The phone began to ring in his hand. Call display said the line was blocked. Was it Renner for her? Was it Seth for him? He hesitated, then offered her the phone.

She leaned over and pushed the button for the speakerphone.

He answered the call. "Hello?"

"Don't talk—just listen." It was Seth. "This call is probably being traced. I mean it's as hidden as I can make it. But we're up against a couple hundred hackers here. Strength in numbers and all that. And I don't have much time before they figure it out—"

Liam's heart rate rose. "Hannah Phillips was kidnapped by Imposters—"

"I know and I told you not to talk." Seth's voice grew urgent. "Go dark. Okay? Really, really dark. No internet. No phones. No people. Definitely no cops. They might shoot you on sight. Assume you're putting anyone you contact in mortal danger just by talking to them. Also, don't let yourself get arrested. I've got no time to explain and don't even know how I would, honestly. Just stay where you are until we figure this out. You're wanted for murder."

The phone went dead. The sound of a dial tone filled the tiny cabin. Kelly watched as the color drained from Liam's face. He stood slowly, still holding Pip. And despite everything that had happened between them, suddenly all she wanted to do was wrap her arms around him and hug him tightly. Instead, she checked the bottle's temperature again and found it was still too cold.

All sorts of words filled her mind, most of which—well, maybe all of which—she knew would be unhelpful. In all the time she'd spent with Liam, she'd almost never seen him thrown off balance or at a loss for words, let alone like things were out of his control. But if she'd remembered anything it was that he needed to be alone inside his own brain to think. For a long moment, neither of them said anything as the wind howled, snow buffeted against the window and Liam jiggled baby Pip in his arms.

"I'll give Pip her bottle," he said. "You lie down and try to get some sleep. I promise I'll wake you up the instant Renner calls or anything happens."

"So we're just going to ignore what Seth said about going dark?" she asked.

"I'm going to take it under advisement," Liam said and his jaw set. "But Seth's not a cop and tends toward exaggeration."

In other words, Liam thought he knew better.

"Now please, get some rest while you can," he said. "You'll need your energy for whatever happens next. You also haven't slept all night and you probably let yourself freeze piloting a speedboat through subzero temperatures, while keeping me and Pip covered by blankets. You apparently kept letting me fall back asleep—"

"You said you needed to sleep it off—" she began.

"You took care of me," Liam said. "Please, let me take care of you and Pip. I promise I won't ditch the phone."

And even as she felt the temptation to be independent and not accept his help, she saw something else in his eyes. He needed this. He needed to take care of her. He needed to do something useful and productive.

Lord, help Liam right now. He looks even more lost than I feel.

"Okay," she said softly. She walked over to him and brushed a kiss over Pip's head, then her hand lingered on his arm. "You'll know the formula is at the right temperature when you don't feel it inside your elbow. She'll complain if it's too cold. I'm pretty sure I won't fall asleep, but I appreciate the chance to lie down."

"Thank you." He nodded. "I've never been the best at knowing the right words to say. But maybe you did make the right call when you took me off that boat. I don't know. But thank you for trying to have my back." Then he broke her gaze and looked down at the baby, but somehow the fingers of Liam's other hand found Kelly's and held them. "And thank you for trusting me with Pip."

She swallowed hard. Her fingers lingered on his for a moment. Then she pulled away and walked over to the couch. It wasn't until she lay down that she realized just how much her entire body ached. She curled onto her side and watched as Liam paced, bouncing Pip gently in his arm and singing something to her softly under his breath. It reminded her of an athlete trying to psych himself up to run onto the field or leap into the ring. For a long moment she just lay there and prayed, not even knowing how to put words to what she was thinking.

To her surprise, sleep swept over her. It was fitful at first, as she went in and out of consciousness like waves lapping on the shore. She was vaguely aware of Pip crying softly and then stopping as Liam fed her. There was the muted sound of Liam's voice as he talked to Pip, to someone on the phone and then to Pip some more, but she couldn't make out the words. Then she heard the sound of Liam singing, his voice a deep and raspy baritone rumble, as he sang a couple of Christmas carols and classic rock-and-roll tunes. It was somewhere during his rendition of "Let Me Call You Sweetheart," mingled with "Baby Love," that she finally fell into a peaceful sleep.

She awoke when she felt the couch shift and opened her eyes to see Liam sitting beside her. The cold blanket that he'd been sleeping under in the boat was now toasty warm, as if he'd laid it over the heater, and was wrapped around her shoulders. The snow had stopped and the sky was dark gray outside the window.

"Hey." His voice was a husky whisper. "Sorry to wake you."

"It's okay." She pulled herself up to sitting. He sat back, but they were so close on the couch their arms brushed and it would've taken nothing for her to lean right into his chest. "Where's Pip?"

"Playing on the floor," he said. She turned. Pip was lying on her back with a pacifier in both hands. "She drank her whole bottle, and I changed her. But she didn't seem to want to go back to sleep."

"She's an incredibly deep sleeper," Kelly said. "Hannah says she can sleep through anything. But on the flip side, when Pip's awake she's wide-awake for a long while. It's like she has an on-off switch." Kelly's arms wrapped around her body and her fingertips brushed his arm. She looked at where her hand sat, barley an inch away from his. "How long was I asleep?"

"Couple of hours," Liam said. "A little less."

"Did Renner call?" she asked.

"No." Liam shook his head. Worry darkened his eyes. "Nor my team. We're no closer to getting any answers and I'm sorry but the phone's battery died." He pressed his hands onto his knees and stood. "It's time we move on. There's no food for us here, we need a phone charger, we'll run out of gas soon and I don't want us to freeze in a shack on an island."

"Me, neither." She also needed more diapers and formula for Pip.

"Thankfully, I was able to get through to a contact of mine before the battery died," Liam went on. "He owns a waterside BBQ restaurant, gas station and motel about half an hour by boat from here. Nothing fancy, but we'll be able to warm up, eat something and charge the phone. Trust me, nobody will find us there. I'm not trying to trap you. I'm just trying to keep you and the baby safe until we sort this out."

She swung her legs over the edge of the couch and ran her fingers through her hair.

"I thought Seth warned you to stay off-the-grid and away from cops," she said.

"He did," Liam said. "My contact isn't a cop. He's a criminal. In a career as long as mine you meet a whole lot of people and sometimes they owe you a favor."

"You're joking," she said.

He wasn't—in fact, he was incredibly serious. His jaw was set, and he was in that focused mode now where he was convinced he'd made the right decision and arguing with him about it wasn't going to work. Her mind might've conveniently edited out those memories about just how big and stubborn a pain in her neck Liam could be, but they were returning to her now.

But you still said yes when he asked you to marry him.

How had she handled this side of him when they were young and in love? She'd let him be focused and do his thing, and then try to talk to him. He'd always listened once he'd completed whatever task was at the top of his mind, and more than half the time he'd agreed with her. And besides, they were short on options. They needed heat, they needed food and she needed to charge her phone. She could always take Pip and go it alone once they got to shore if she didn't like how things were playing out.

But just because something wasn't the worst possible option didn't make it a good one.

They cleaned the cottage, left some money under one of the candles and changed Pip one last time before they left. Both the snow and wind had died down. The sky was a lighter shade of gray now, with just the smallest wisps of pink brushing the very edges. She wrapped Pip up in a cocoon-type sleeping bag that all but engulfed her and buckled her into her car seat.

It took them over half an hour to slowly maneuver the motorboat down the St. Lawrence River, traveling east. The river was so deep and wide it usually didn't freeze over until the very end of January, and even then icebreakers were usually deployed to keep parts of it open. Still, the air was so cold it seemed to nip at her skin and thick ice was already building around the island shorelines. Between the intense cold, the sound of the motor and the rushing wind, she gave up trying to discuss Liam's plan further until he pulled the boat to a stop in a small marina on the Canadian mainland.

She looked around. A sprawling waterside restaurant stretched along the shoreline with a huge snow-covered deck overhanging the water. There were four docks, with space for twenty-five to thirty motorboats, a gas station for both vehicles and boats and a small convenience store that advertised ice, Popsicles and worms. According to a sign, there were motel rooms over the restaurant as well as cabins and camping space. Several signs that read Sorry, Closed for the Season dotted the windows. According to huge red-and-blue lettering, the whole place was straightforwardly named Bill's BBQ, Motel and Gas.

Liam docked the boat, climbed out and reached back for her. She slung the diaper bag over her shoulder, took hold of the car seat and climbed out onto the dock. Pip had just fallen asleep in the last fifteen minutes and hopefully she'd sleep for a while. The wood was slippery. Dark water rushed beneath them.

"So I take it your contact's name is Bill?" she asked.

"That's one of his names, yeah," Liam said. "Bill Leckie is what I think he's going by now. Before that it was William Hancock, Stephen Griggs, Harlow Daly and Gilbert Petticrew, among others." Liam shrugged. "He's been around a long time."

None of this was filling her with confidence. He turned slightly, like he was ready to head to the restaurant. But when she instead stood there on the dock and stretched, he stayed put.

"You said he was a criminal?" she asked. "What kind of criminal?"

"He...moves things," Liam said. "Or at least he used to. He acquires things and transports them, often across borders."

"Like weapons?" she asked.

"Nah," Liam said. "Pills and medications. There's a huge black market for cheap pharmaceuticals, especially considering different things are legal in Canada and the States. Convinced himself he was helping people. By the third time I'd arrested him, he'd gotten smart and realized it was easiest to plead guilty, take a lesser punishment and point me toward someone worse than him. He eventually started keeping his work low-key and doing more informant work for me. He claims he's gone completely legit and is in retirement."

Again, he turned to walk up toward the building, and once again she didn't budge. It was hardly her fault he hadn't felt things were up for discussion and that they hadn't been able to talk on the boat due to the wind and noise. Fact was, now that she and Pip were here, there really wasn't any reason why she couldn't just leave Liam to sort things out on his own while she and Pip tried to make their own way, somehow. The sun would be up soon. And sure, she didn't have a phone charger, a cell signal or a plan, and she was down to one final diaper change and meal for Pip. But she still had some cash, not to mention her wits.

"At the risk of sounding like a cliché," she said, "I've got a really bad feeling about this. The place looks abandoned and something about it is giving me the jitters."

"I don't blame you," Liam said. "But it's okay. Bill owes me a favor."

"What kind of favor could a former pharmaceutical drug smuggler owe you?" she asked.

"A big one," Liam said.

He turned for a third time to step off the frozen dock and head toward the building. But this time her hand darted out and grabbed his.

"Not good enough," she said.

He turned back, his eyes met hers and then he looked down at her hand holding his.

"Bill has a daughter," he said slowly. "Her name is Emily. She's six. She's his whole entire life and the reason he retired. Bill made a lot of mistakes in his life and then when he thought his life was over he was suddenly surprised to have some precious little person who needed him and loved him. A few months ago some people with an ax to grind kidnapped her. They threatened to hurt her. Bill called me. I had her back to him, unharmed and safe, by dinnertime."

He looked at the sleeping baby for a long moment. Then he looked back up at Kelly and his dark eyes met hers.

"The guys who kidnapped her are in jail now and will be for a very long time," he added. "My dad always told me that when you dedicated yourself to a rough life, surrounded by bad people, any kind of close relationship was a risk. It could throw you off your game and put the people you love in danger."

"I remember," she said.

Somehow she suspected it was the only one of his father's tactical tips Liam had ever gotten close to breaking. He stepped back and his hand slowly, almost reluctantly, fell from hers.

"Anyway, Bill owes me a favor," Liam said. A wry smile turned at the corner of one lip on one side of his mouth. "So I told him that my former old lady was back, with a grandkid she said was mine, and we needed a place to hide."

She took in a sharp and icy breath.

"He knows I like to keep my life private," Liam said, "and that I've got a reputation within the RCMP that doesn't include having a secret grandchild due to an ill-advised, against-protocol relationship I had with someone I placed in witness protection. I might've even been kicked off the force. My career would've tanked then if news of what had happened between us had gotten out. Even now, despite whatever else is going on here, I could still face a disciplinary hearing over my past relationship with you or some kind of negative consequences to my reputation and career. But, Bill will have my back. Like I said, he owes me. Now come on, he's probably in there waiting for us."

He turned and walked toward the restaurant, so quickly and firmly she couldn't have grabbed his hand again if she'd wanted to. She followed him up the stairs and across the deck—the empty deck with its picnic tables inches deep in snow. He reached for the door, found it unlocked and pushed it open. They stepped into the restaurant. It was empty and dark. Chairs were stacked upside down on empty tables.

As the door clicked shut behind them, a young man in a thick beard stepped out from behind it and pressed the barrel of a gun to the side of Liam's head.

"Down on your knees." The voice was low and mean. His face was lost in shadows and the click of the gun was unmistakable. "You're about to learn what happens to someone who tries to lie to Bill Leckie, and it ain't going to be pretty."

SEVEN

"You tell Bill, I didn't cross him," Liam
said calmly, raising his hands, "and I
await his apology when he figures that
out. Now, tell me, what exactly does Bill
think I've done?"

Then, before the man could even formu-
late an answer, Liam struck, apparently
more interested in distracting his attacker
long enough to get the upper hand than
hearing what he had to say. Kelly watched
as Liam spun toward the gun-wielding
man, grabbing the weapon before he could
even fire and slamming him into the wall.
She felt a gust of wind and heard the door
slam and click shut again. She blinked.
Liam had disarmed his attacker, thrown
him out and locked the door behind him,

without even breaking a sweat. Then she felt Liam's strong hand on her shoulder, guiding her and the still-sleeping baby underneath a table, sheltering them with his body.

"Stay here," Liam whispered, his voice urgent. His face was just inches from hers. Worry flooded his eyes. "It's an ambush. That guy won't be alone and just because I was able to catch him off guard doesn't mean the others won't put up more of a fight." Not to mention the guy he just locked outside would be trying to get back in, no doubt. "There are other doors to this place, but we'd have to go through the kitchen or down the hallway, both of which are risky. This is an easier place to defend. Whatever Bill thinks I've done, he won't want his goons hurting you or the baby. He's got way too much honor than to allow a woman or child to get hurt on his watch, and has probably already told his attack dogs to leave you alone. I'm the one they're after. I'll get you out of here.

Just promise me, if you get a clear path to escape, just take Pip and go, okay? Don't wait for me and don't look back."

Before she could answer, his hand slid to the side of her face. His lips brushed over her forehead. Then he rolled back out into the room and leaped to his feet, knocking a table in front of Kelly and Pip's hiding space as he did so, further shielding and protecting them.

"Like I told Bill, I have a woman and baby with me!" he shouted to the seemingly empty room. He tucked the gun he'd lifted into his belt. "If you're Bill's men you'll know full well that hurting innocent women and children is against his code. Whatever his problem is, it's with me, not them. And no weapon fire, please. The kid's asleep and Bill won't want you making things loud and scaring her awake."

He sounded so calm and in control, as if he was the only person there who really understood what was going on. Kelly slid Pip's car seat into the corner against the wall, sheltering it with her body and praying God would protect Pip from realizing they were in danger. Then Kelly crouched up onto the balls of her feet and looked out through gaps in the chairs and fallen table that barricaded her from view. As she watched, two more men, of varying heights, wearing plaid jackets and with full-length beards, stepped out of the shadows. Liam had been so convinced that Bill would protect them and he'd been wrong.

Lord, please keep us safe.

She watched as Liam raised his badge high.

"I'm Liam Bearsmith!" he shouted at the approaching men. "RCMP. Stand down! Now! Or I'll arrest you for assaulting an officer."

The taller of the two men chuckled. The other swore and told Liam in colorful language he was about to hurt him.

"Well," Liam said, "it was worth a shot."

And then, it was as if everything was

happening at once. He dove and rolled behind a table on the far side of the room, disappearing from view and drawing the men away from her hiding spot. The men charged toward him. He leaped up and tossed a chair high in the air toward them. Somebody fired and the chair exploded, sending splinters raining down around them. Pip whimpered in her sleep. But Liam was already on the move, somehow coming up from behind the man who'd fired. He wrenched the weapon from his grasp and delivered a blow to his jaw that sent him to the ground. A gust of cold wind dragged her attention toward the kitchen. The man whom Liam had tossed outside had apparently run around the building, come in the front and was back to join the fray. Did that mean the coast was now clear outside again?

If she grabbed Pip and made a run for it, out the back door, would she make it? Did she really want to run without Liam? No. Somehow, she knew she didn't.

Please, Lord, get Liam and I out of this together.

The second man charged toward Liam now with his weapon raised. But Liam got to this one before he could even fire, catching him around the middle, and tossed him to the ground. Just one attacker left, and this one seemed determined to take Liam, dead or alive. He roared in anger, raising his weapon and firing, again and again, as Liam dodged and rolled out of the line of fire as if somehow his body knew just where every bullet was about to land. Windows shattered. Pictures cracked. Pip awoke with a howl. The weapon clicked. Liam's attacker was out of bullets and Liam was on him, sweeping out his legs with a roundhouse kick before he could even reload.

"When Bill comes groveling for this, I'm telling him you're the one who woke my grandkid," Liam said. He bent down and grabbed something from the man's pocket. Then he turned and ran for Kelly.

He slid to a stop beside her hiding place, bent down on one knee and reached for her hand.

"Come on," he said. "This is when we run."

Kelly felt him grab her hand. With his other hand, Liam grabbed Pip's car seat, and almost immediately the baby's tears faded.

"Sorry, girl," Liam told Pip. "We're getting you somewhere quiet right now."

Kelly glanced toward Liam's attackers, who were now groaning on the floor, but Liam tugged her hand.

"Trust me," he said. "They'll be okay. Let's go."

They ran outside, leaving the shambles of the diner behind. They raced from the diner, past the convenience store and into a parking lot.

"Stay close!" Liam shouted. He dropped her hand and reached into his pocket, and then she realized what he'd taken from the third attacker. It was a set of car keys.

He pointed them at the closest car and clicked the remote key fob. Nothing happened. Just as swiftly, he yanked the gun from his waist and shot out one of the vehicle's tires.

"Not that one," he said, as if to himself.

Two more cars and a truck lay ahead. He clicked the fob at each of them. No response. He shot out one of each of their tires, as well. Then the lights flashed on a black four-door truck ahead on their right. It was sturdy, with four-wheel drive and snow tires. Liam whispered a prayer of thanks under his breath. "That's our ride."

They ran for it. He yanked open the back door and she tumbled in with Pip.

He leaped in the front and waited as she buckled Pip's car seat in and then climbed in the front. The moment her seat belt was buckled, he hit the gas. The vehicle shot forward, swerved out of the parking lot and onto the road. She glanced back. Men were stumbling out of the restaurant into the parking lot after them, and Pip was already falling back asleep.

"I'm so sorry about that," Liam said. "I have no clue what that was about, but I promise you I'll find out." He glanced over his shoulder at Pip and then back to Kelly. His right hand reached for hers and took it, linking her fingers through his. "Are you okay? Is she okay? You weren't hit by splinters or anything?"

"We're okay," Kelly said softly. "We're both okay."

"Are you sure?" His voice was oddly husky. Something tender rumbled in its depths. And despite everything that had happened back at the restaurant, something made her suspect what upset him the most was the fact he'd put her and Pip in danger.

"I'm sure," she said. She squeezed his hand, letting her fingers run over his, and something tightened in her chest. "We're okay. Shaken up but not injured."

He whispered a prayer of thanks to God.

Then he stared straight ahead down the empty road as the sun rose higher over the snowy tree line. His hand hadn't left hers and neither of them pulled away.

"Is your favorite getaway vehicle still a white truck?" Kelly asked.

His eyebrows rose. "White because it gets dirty fast and so is often overlooked," he said, almost to himself, "and a truck for maneuverability, yeah... I'm surprised you remembered."

"I remember a lot," she said.

"Yeah, so do I."

Then he pulled away his hand and something inside her missed the feel of it. Deep lines furrowed his brow. She glanced over her shoulder. So far, it looked like they weren't being followed. Then again, Liam had shot a few tires.

"Okay, so let's recap," Liam said. "Now Bill thinks I'm lying to him about something. He sends his guys after me. But doesn't come personally. So he expected they'd be able to handle me without much trouble."

There was something routine about the way he said it, as if being ambushed and having his life threatened was something he was used to. It was a little bit impressive and incredibly sad. His jaw was set so tightly it was almost clenched.

"And again," he added. "I have no idea why. But I'm going to find out."

"How?" she asked.

"I don't know yet."

Liam fell silent. The icy road spread out white ahead of them. Snow-covered trees were tinged with shadows and gray in the early morning light. For a long time he didn't say anything, and neither did she, and when she glanced at Pip she saw the baby had fallen asleep. Questions, worries and fears cascaded through her mind. Why hadn't Renner messaged her before her phone died? Was Hannah okay? Why had the cop on the boat tried to arrest Liam and why had Liam's contact, Bill, sent criminals after him? Why had both called Liam a liar?

Who'd doctored her witness-protection file and kept them apart?

Why had God allowed the man she'd once loved to crash back into her life now?

The sun rose higher, lightening the gray around them. They passed a tiny town and then a second, both barely more than a handful of buildings and a momentary speed-limit change. Tension was building inside her. She needed a phone charger. They needed food. They'd eventually need gas for the vehicle they were in, which was most definitely stolen, or a new set of wheels. More than anything, she needed information. But getting anything out of Liam was like chipping at a stone.

"So let me try the recap thing," she said. Worked for him, so she might as well try it. "Seth told you not to trust police, and after what happened with the cop on the boat, that makes sense. But based on what happened with Bill, maybe you can't trust criminal contacts, either. Renner hasn't contacted me, Hannah's been kidnapped by the Imposters and neither of us have been able to get online for almost twelve hours, so we have no actual idea what's going on in the outside world. We need food, diapers, a phone charger and a quiet, warm and safe place to lay low. Am I missing anything?"

"I'm supposed to be at a wedding some-time today," Liam said dryly, "and another one tomorrow."

"Two weddings in two days?" Kelly asked.

"Three weddings in eight." Liam cast her a sideways glance. "Every detective on the team but me is getting married over the holidays."

He nodded at something on the empty road ahead and even as she followed his gaze it took her a moment to see it. Parked ahead, half-hidden in the trees, was an Ontario Provincial Police car, its white doors dingy with snow.

She watched his lips move as if taking stock for himself.

"Speed trap," he said. "One cop. OPP. Routine traffic duty. Likely a rookie. Here we go."

"What does that mean?" she asked.

"I'm going to get myself arrested."

He was what? But before she could even argue, Liam gunned the engine, revving it so quickly she felt the vehicle lurch beneath her. He began to accelerate, pushing the vehicle faster and faster as they sped past the police car.

Its lights flashed and its sirens blared. She glanced back as the cop pulled onto the road and came after them.

Liam's eyes cut to the mirror.

"Okay," Liam said. "He'll sit behind us in his car for a moment and run the plates. He probably won't call for backup. Considering this truck belongs to one of Bill's men, he's unlikely to report it stolen, because Bill's never been one to get the police involved when he can avoid it. He'd rather write the vehicle off. At least my hope is that's the case and that this truck isn't linked to a crime. If all goes well, the cop will walk over here and ticket me."

Liam pulled over to the side of the long, empty highway. The cop pulled over behind him. Liam turned to Kelly.

"You've got money, right?" Liam asked, his eyes intense and intent on hers. "Stun gun? A way to contact Renner once you charge your phone?"

"Yes." She nodded. She had all of that. But what about Liam?

"Here's what's going to happen," Liam said. "I'm going to draw him away from the car. He's going to arrest me and I'm going to let it happen. No, don't argue. I know the inner workings of law enforcement better than anyone, I know how to get answers and the name 'Detective Liam Bearsmith' still counts for something, despite what Seth might think I should do. There's only one of him so he can't detain us both and I'll be sure to tell him that you had nothing to do with this. You're going to wait until you see him handcuffing me, then go find a safe place to hide and lay low. Get rid of the car. Get a phone charger and contact Renner. I know you can do it. And I will find a way to get in touch as soon as I can. And maybe, we can meet up."

But, maybe not?

He glanced back. The cop had gotten out of his vehicle and was walking toward them. There was no time to argue. No time to find another plan.

Liam looked at her. "Goodbye, sweethea—" he began, but his voice caught on the last syllable like he'd just realized what he'd said. "I'm sorry."

"Don't be," she said. "You can call me that whenever you want."

And then, she kissed him.

It wasn't the first time someone had unexpectedly tried to kiss Liam Bearsmith. When he'd told Kelly the day before she'd been the only woman he'd ever kissed, that had been completely and entirely true. He hadn't so much as held another woman in his arms or even held her hand. But during his myriad undercover assignments, pretending to be a bodyguard or thug, people he was either targeting or rescuing had occasionally tried and failed to embrace him, which had always been awkward and uncomfortable, and not the slightest bit pleasant or welcomed. But this was definitely the one and only time, in over twenty years, that he'd ever kissed a woman back.

Time froze. Logically, he knew the fleeting kiss must've only lasted seconds. But there was something almost indescribable about feeling Kelly's lips brush his. It was warm and comforting. It was like coming home to a place he'd missed, or finding something he'd lost far too long ago.

No, it was like he was the one who was being found, when he hadn't even known he'd been lost.

They broke the kiss, he got out of the car and started toward the cop now walking toward him and for the first time in a long time, Liam felt an unfamiliar feeling grinding inside him. *Doubt.* Something about this whole plan he'd just concocted felt wrong. Really wrong. Yes, Seth had warned him off contacting anyone in law enforcement. But considering Liam's complete and total lack of a phone right now, getting taken in was a very effective way for him to pull rank, flex his muscles and take charge of the situation. It just made sense.

So then why did it feel like his heart was getting chewed up inside a set of invisible gears? The cop drew closer. He couldn't leave Kelly and Pip. Not without making sure they were safe. And while he was mostly sure that everything would be okay if Kelly and Pip were taken into custody by law enforcement, the number of unusual things that had happened in the past few hours gnawed at him. What if they thought Kelly had committed a crime and arrested her? What if they took Pip away from Kelly? How long would it take to get Kelly and her granddaughter reunited? Sure, he'd given Kelly his word the night before that he'd be able to make sure everything went smoothly for her and she was taken care of, but now after everything, how could he really be sure?

Help me, Lord. What's this thing inside me? What's it trying to tell me?

He'd failed Kelly once. He couldn't fail her again.

"Good morning, sir," the cop called. "I'm going to have to ask you to get back in your truck."

Which was protocol to avoid anyone getting hit by a passing car. Liam respected him for that. Not that every officer would worry about it on a road this desolate. Liam eyed the man, taking in all the information he could with a glance. He was young, maybe twenty-five, with a polite and professional voice and the kind of build that implied his strength wasn't just a temporary side effect of youth. He was someone who'd either volunteered for an incredibly boring, bone-chillingly cold side-of-the-road duty in the early morning that most cops would do anything to avoid, or he didn't have enough seniority to avoid it. He wasn't much older than Hannah, so was young enough to be his son.

"Get back in your car, sir," the officer repeated. "And if you'd be so kind to get your license and registration out for me."

Liam glanced back over his shoulder at Kelly. And a prayer filled his heart as his eyes met hers. *Help me, Lord. What do I do?* He could put Kelly in danger by getting her arrested, or leave her to fend on her own, or make this cop's life a whole lot harder. And he never liked making a good cop's life difficult.

He turned back to the cop. The young man's hand reached for his weapon, but his tone remained both firm and polite.

"I said, get back in your truck."

Lord, forgive me for what I'm about to do.

Liam turned and ran.

"Hey!" the cop yelled. "Stop!"

Oh, he would, Liam thought, as soon as he figured out what his game plan was. For now, he was buying himself all the time he could. Liam raised his hands high, showing the cop pursuing him that he was unarmed. Liam passed the car, putting as much distance between himself and it as possible. The idea that he could evade this cop, give Kelly a chance to drive off and then double back and find her again crossed his mind. Then another realization hit him. The young man was actually gaining on him. This man could possibly outrun him. For the first time in his life, the great Liam Bearsmith was actually about to be outrun and taken down by a younger, fitter cop. Huh. Well, that narrowed his options. There was only one thing left—he had to put his trust in the training, dedication and innate goodness of the men and women in blue he'd served alongside his entire career and pray the man behind him now was no exception.

"Sorry, change of plan!" Liam called. "I'm surrendering!"

Before he could turn, the cop launched into him, tackling Liam hard from behind and forcing him down on the ground. The two men tumbled and Liam rolled clumsily, clutching the other man as if to steady himself in a move he hoped looked more accidental than intentional.

"I'm sorry!" Liam said. His hand brushed the cop's shoulder. "I'm really, really sorry."

And he was, especially for everything that was about to happen next.

The young man leaped to his feet, instinctively checking that his gun was secure, but missing the fact Liam had just disabled his radio.

The man stepped back, pulled his

weapon and aimed it at Liam with both hands.

"Stay down!" The cop's voice rose. "Hands up!"

Textbook, Liam thought admiringly. He crouched on the balls of his feet and raised his hands.

"I'm sorry," Liam said again, "but you would not believe the night I had. People keep trying to either kill me, drug me, shoot at me or arrest me. It's been crazy. I know I should've stayed in the vehicle, but there's an innocent woman and infant in there, and I wanted to get them as far away from me and my mess as possible. I really don't want anyone getting hurt because of me."

"Nobody's going to get hurt," the cop replied and while his weapon didn't waver an inch, Liam could tell the young man was actually listening. Yeah, Liam was definitely going to recommend him for a promotion when this whole mess was cleared. "Now, again, I need to see your license and registration."

"I don't have it!" Liam called. "I was robbed at gunpoint a few hours ago by masked criminals who took it. They took everything, except my police badge. Run the number, I'm Detective Liam Bearsmith, RCMP. And you're OPP, right?"

Something flickered behind the young man's eyes, but all he said was, "Constable Jake Marlie, Ontario Provincial Police, Thousand Islands Detachment."

Liam snorted. "Marley, like the Christmas ghost?"

"No, Marlie like the Toronto hockey team."

"Can I call you Jake?" Liam asked.

"No." Constable Marlie shook his head. "Now, tell me again, what's your name?"

"I already told you," Liam said. "But clearly you don't believe me! Which isn't new. So how about you tell me why nobody believes I'm who I say I am?"

Constable Marlie didn't answer. Instead he turned his head toward his radio and called for backup, shooting off police codes rapid-fire. There was 10-33, 10-35, 10-62, 10-26 and 10-64—which basically summed up as "come help me quick, there's a major crime alert about a possible suspect who needs to be detained quickly—proceed with caution." Marlie added 10-93—calling for a roadblock. Then Marlie's brow furrowed. He'd realized his radio wasn't working.

Lord, help me de-escalate this before it gets out of hand.

"Get down!" Constable Marlie yelled. "On the ground. Hands behind your head."

There was a click and Liam watched as the truck door opened behind him and Kelly stepped out. The early morning light caught her features, illuminating her form in an almost ethereal glow.

"Get back in the truck!" Liam called.

But she ignored him and instead focused on the officer.

"Hey, Constable!" Kelly yelled. "Mind

telling me why nobody believes him when he tells them who he is?"

Constable Marlie spun.

"Ma'am," he shouted and his voice rose. "Get back in the vehicle! Now!"

"I can't do that," Kelly shouted. "Not until somebody explains what's going on. You're going to have to arrest me first."

And something snapped inside Liam like a rubber band that had been stretched too far returning back to its normal length. He leaped, catching Constable Marlie's arm, and then wrestled the weapon from his hands. Then he marched Marlie back to the truck and pushed him against the hood of the truck, as if he was the uniformed cop and Marlie was the suspect.

"Don't worry," Liam said. "I'm not going to hurt you. I promise. You're a good cop and I respect that. I'm just going to cuff you with your own handcuffs long enough for us to talk and sort this out. And then I'm going to let you go."

He wrenched the cop's hands behind his back and cuffed them.

"I feel really bad about this," Liam added. "Don't take it personally. Because as one cop to another, I can tell you that you did everything by the book. I've just got like two decades experience on you and an encyclopedic knowledge of how you do our job. That's all."

Then he turned the constable around and stepped back.

"When this mess is all cleared up and I file my police report about this," Liam added, "I'll make sure it reflects your professionalism and recommends you for promotion. I'm genuinely impressed."

Although, it was clear by the look in the cop's eyes he wasn't much impressed with Liam and didn't believe a word he was saying.

"Now, please, tell me why people keep trying to kill me and don't believe me when I tell them who I am?" Liam asked.

"Liam Bearsmith is dead," Constable

Marlie said bluntly. Then despite all obvious evidence to the contrary, he added, "And you're under arrest for his murder."

EIGHT

She watched as Liam startled, like his whole being was shaken by the news. Then he stepped back and offered his own hand to help the cuffed constable stand. Liam opened his mouth but no words came out, and he closed it again. He looked up to the sky in what she guessed was either silent prayer, processing or both. Then finally he turned back to the officer.

"Well, that's a new one," Liam said. "First of all, Constable Marlie, total respect for trying to tell me that I was under arrest when you were the one in handcuffs. You remind me of myself at your age, and I mean that as a compliment. Secondly, and I can't believe I'm saying this, but I'm not dead and I'm not my own murderer. So why would you possibly think I was?"

Constable Marlie didn't even blink—instead, his chin rose.

"Let's start with the fact it's all over the news," Marlie said. "The cruise ship had security cameras, plus people posted videos online. There's clear footage of your... of Bearsmith's death, including you shooting him—"

"Me?" Liam interrupted.

"A man who looks similar enough to Bearsmith to pass for him," Constable Marlie explained as he turned to Kelly, "but who clearly isn't the same man if you look closely enough. This man not only killed the RCMP officer, he stole his identity. There's a nationwide warrant out for his arrest. Divers are searching Lake Ontario for his body. So I don't know when the actual funeral will be. But there's going to be a candlelight vigil for the real Liam Bearsmith in Ottawa tonight at seven. Police officers are coming from across Canada to attend."

Then Constable Marlie's eyes cut back to Liam and something hardened in their depths.

"This man's name is Steve Parker," he said. "He looks similar enough to Bearsmith, but if you put pictures of him and Bearsmith side by side it's easy enough to tell them apart. This man's a bit shorter, heavier set and the shape of his face and nose are different."

Kelly felt her eyebrows rise. Liam rocked back on his heels and let out a long breath.

"Steve Parker is one of my deep covers," he said. A rumble almost like a roar was building in the back of his throat. "Last used him about eighteen months ago."

He ran both hands over his face as if trying to wipe away his former cover. Then he turned to Kelly.

"You know I'm really me, right?" he asked her. And she was surprised to see how much doubt filled his eyes. "I know I look different than I used to. I mean, I know it's been over twenty years and I probably don't look anything like you remember. I'm a lot older and battle-worn. I've got a few more scars, I'm nowhere near as fit as I used to be and my nose has been literally bent out of shape."

"Stop it," Kelly said firmly. "Of course I know who you are. You're you, and you're perfect at it."

His eyes widened. Okay, she wasn't sure why *perfect* was the word she'd blurted out. Her hand brushed his jaw and she felt him shiver slightly under her touch.

"I know you, Liam," she went on. "You're the same stubborn, driven, too-independent-for-your-own-good, cop-through-and-through man that you've always been."

Suddenly she remembered how natural it had felt when she'd spontaneously kissed him. And how he'd kissed her back.

She stepped back and looked at Constable Marlie.

"Obviously heard of the Imposters?" she demanded. "You know, the slew of young men in masks and eye patches who took over the boat?" The look on Constable Marlie's face didn't confirm much of an answer one way or the other. She pressed on. "The Imposters are cyber-criminals. The original two died last year after stealing the RCMP's witness-protection database and trying to auction it off to criminals online. Now this new bunch have sprung up. Can you imagine how impossible it is to take out an organization with no leader or set goals? I can't. They're threatening global chaos." *They kidnapped our daughter!* "They're behind this. And we have to stop them. That's all that matters."

She heard the sound of a vehicle rumbling softly up the empty and desolate road toward them. Instinctively, it seemed,

Liam stepped between them and the passing car to shield them from view.

"Come on," Liam said, his voice thick with an emotion she couldn't place. "Let's see what we can find out, quickly, and then get out of Constable Marlie's hair and let him go on his way. Thankfully, several sectors of law enforcement have implemented an automated fingerprint-identification system. All I've got to do is run my fingerprints through it and it'll prove who I am."

It was such an incredibly simple and almost anticlimactic solution that there was something comforting about it. Less than five minutes later, Kelly was sitting in the back of Constable Marlie's patrol car with the door wide open, to allay her fear of getting locked in, and baby Pip reluctantly awake again and bouncing on her lap.

Liam sat in the driver's seat, with the still-handcuffed Constable Marlie in the passenger seat. She was frankly amazed at how Marlie had been mostly listening and observing. Had she been in the constable's shoes, she would have been alternating between shouting the place down and asking nonstop questions. But Marlie seemed focused on listening and taking in as much information as possible. She suspected Liam would've done the same.

She held her breath as Liam scanned his own fingerprints and ran them through the police's automated fingerprint-identification system, comparing them to the ones on file for Liam Bearsmith. Then she watched as the color drained from his face.

"They're not a match," Liam said. He looked back at her over his shoulder. "They changed my fingerprints. Somebody actually hacked into my official RCMP police file and changed my fingerprints." He scanned the laptop screen and his scowl deepened. "My height, my age, my weight, even my official photo— they've all been tweaked. Somebody actually hacked into my official file and tried to get rid of me."

He let out a hard breath and stuttered some unintelligible syllables under his breath, like he was trying to make words but his tongue was failing.

"Somebody changed my official witness-protection file, too," she reminded him.

To make it look like I was married to drive us apart. And then that I was dead.

Liam turned to the constable.

"How do I find this video footage that apparently shows a version of me killing me?" he asked. "Where exactly is it?"

"The internet," the cop said dryly, with just the slightest tinge of sarcasm in his voice, as if he'd just stopped himself from calling Liam "Grandpa." "It's literally all over the internet. You just need to put your name in a search engine and it will come up."

Your name, Kelly noted.

Liam did so, found an entire page's

worth of videos and clicked the first one. A shaky video appeared, with bad audio and low-res graphics. There was a younger, fitter and stronger version of Liam Bearsmith kneeling on the deck of the boat with his hands raised, looking so movie-star impressive he might as well have been airbrushed. There was a tired, older, shivering, wet and exhausted-looking Liam, who looked a lot more like the man now sitting in front of her, taking Superstar Liam's wallet and badge before holding a gun to his head and shooting him. Superstar Liam collapsed in a pool of blood. Tired Liam turned and looked directly at the camera.

"Well...that..." Liam shook his head. She glanced at him in the rearview mirror. Any remaining vestiges of blood fled his face, leaving his skin as ashen as the dirty snow outside. "That...is... I... Wow..."

"It's what's called a deep fake," Kelly said quickly. "They use computer-generated images and digitally altered existing footage to create this. It's not real."

Then a stray and disconcerting thought crossed her mind. She'd never asked Hannah how she knew for sure Renner was alive and that it was him communicating with her. Could that have been faked, as well? Could he really have created a master-key decryption device and been killed for it, and it had been somebody else pretending to be him to lure Hannah into danger?

"If I didn't know any better I'd think a younger and stronger version of myself traveled through time and I killed him," Liam said wearily.

"Yeah, that's the point," Kelly said, forcing her worrying thoughts aside for a moment. "Judging by the time stamp, it was posted online minutes before that cop tried to arrest you on the boat. Which might explain why he was so off his game, if he'd just gotten word you had a murderous doppelgänger on the loose. I'm guessing that's also why Seth told you to go dark and a man whose daughter you saved sent goons to kill you. Guess the downside of being famous and beloved is that everyone wants to help avenge your murder."

"I'm neither of those things," Liam muttered. He turned to Constable Marlie. "And this is all over the internet?"

"And television," Marlie said. "It's the top trending story on all the major socialmedia sites. It's international news."

Liam pressed his lips together and nodded slowly.

"Well, Kelly," he said. "Seems you were right about thinking we should've gotten online as soon as possible." He really was waking up to a whole new world. One where he was both dead and wanted for murder. "How do we get this off the internet and prove that I'm not dead and not an evil double who murdered the real me, before the next person we run into isn't as professional as Constable Jake Marlie here and instead has a shoot-first, ask-questions-second mentality?"

"With a lot of difficulty," she admitted, "and a lot of help."

She watched as Liam closed his eyes and a silent prayer crossed his lips. Then he turned to Constable Marlie.

"You're a great cop from what I've seen and I don't want to do anything to hurt your career," Liam said. "If I give you the key, do you know how to get your hands free from the cuffs?" Marlie shook his head. "Well, it's a good skill to learn, and I'll cuff one hand to the steering wheel instead to make it easier. Then I'll leave you with the key, let the air out of your tires and go. By the time you radio for help and they get here, we'll be gone."

"Look," Constable Marlie began, "I don't know what's going on and I'm not saying I'm convinced you're Liam Bearsmith but—"

Liam held up a hand to silence him.

"No," he said. "I'm Steve Parker, or whoever. That's all you know. You stick with that. Because if I was Liam Bearsmith, the last thing I'd want or need right now is for whoever's behind this to think that I have a clue what's going on. I'd want them to think I'm clueless. And I also wouldn't want a good cop taking collateral damage over this, either. Got it?"

The constable nodded.

Liam turned to Kelly. "Take Pip back to the truck and get her buckled in. I'll meet you there in five."

She did as he asked, saying a quick goodbye to Constable Marlie because it felt wrong to just walk away without saying something. True to his word, Liam met her back at the truck four minutes later.

"Thanks to the constable's computer, I've confirmed that law enforcement have mounted a full-scale operation to locate and rescue Hannah," he said as he slid back into the driver's seat. He closed the door and did up his seat belt. "The good news is that she appears to be safe and unharmed for now. The Imposters have been posting about her online, offering to trade her safe return for Renner's decryption key."

"But Renner hasn't responded, has he?" she asked.

Liam shook his head. "No, why?"

"Because almost all of Hannah's communication with Renner has been typing," she said. "They've only had a few quick video calls. What if you were right? What if Renner is dead and it was all faked? What if no one was ever going to message me back?"

Liam reached for her hand and squeezed it. "She's alive, and we're going to find her. That's all that matters right now." He glanced over his shoulder at the baby in the back in her car seat.

"Restless," Kelly said. "Along with needing food and a steady supply of fresh diapers, I'm worried she's not getting enough time to stretch and move. She's very wriggly. Even babies this little need time to play."

"Understood," Liam said. He pulled out onto the road and started driving.

Her eyes glanced to the clock. It was almost eight in the morning and had been less than eleven hours since she'd bumped into Liam back on the Toronto docks.

"I feel bad for Constable Marlie," Liam said after a long moment.

"He knew it was you," Kelly said. "Not at first, but by the end you'd convinced him."

"Maybe," Liam said. "When this is all sorted I'll make sure his career doesn't take a hit for this."

"For arresting the incomparable Liam Bearsmith when he was on the run under false charges?" Kelly asked. "Or for the fact a suspected criminal overpowered him and handcuffed him?"

"A bit of both," Liam said. "Maybe more A than B."

He was quiet for a long moment. Her

eyes gazed over at the impossibly incredible and handsome man, whom she felt closer to than she'd ever felt to anyone else, and yet in some ways who still felt like a stranger. His brow was furrowed. He'd been willing to throw away a career in law enforcement for her, and now his dedication to it was so strong he was worried about the junior-level officer who'd tried to arrest him.

Maybe it had been right he'd ended up in the RCMP instead of with her.

Liam turned toward her, as if sensing her eyes on his face. "Do you want to go to a wedding?"

Detective Jessica Eddington stood alone in the tiny study of the apartment on the second floor of Tatlow's Used Books in the small town of Kilpatrick, Ontario. Jess looked somewhat like a fairy-tale princess, Liam thought as he cautiously stepped foot onto the freezing second-floor fire-escape platform and continued to watch her through the window, to ensure she was actually alone. Her long blond hair was somehow both piled on top of her head and falling in loose waves around her shoulders, and the white cape that draped over her white wedding dress seemed to fall in glittery waves all the way to the floor. Jess spun toward the window, yanked her weapon from somewhere inside the shimmering fabric and aimed it straight between his eyes.

Liam's hands rose.

"Jess!" He hissed. "It's me! Liam! I'm—I'm not dead."

But he'd barely gotten a handful of words into his rambling explanation when the bride dropped the weapon back into some hidden pocket in her dress, ran across the study and yanked open the window.

"Liam!" A delighted smile burst across her face, like a little sister welcoming her brother home from college. "Come in! Get in!"

Despite being half his size, pretty much,

she practically yanked him through the window.

"I'm not dead," he said again.

"I know!" She laughed. "Now get in before anyone sees you."

"Did Seth fill you in on the situation?" he asked.

Jess's eyes widened. "I haven't heard from Seth in hours. He was supposed to be one of our witnesses, but then he sent a text to both Travis and I in the middle of the night saying he wouldn't make it to the wedding. According to Travis, Willow isn't that happy with him over it."

No, Liam didn't think she would be. Six-year-old Willow definitely had strong opinions about things and was a force to be reckoned with. Seth had grown close to former detective Travis Tatlow, his adopted daughter, Willow, and her baby brother, Dominic, when Seth and Jess had gone undercover to help them escape deadly criminals from Travis's past last June.

What could possibly be serious enough to make Seth miss Travis and Jess's wedding?

"Mack, Noah and I did touch base about you briefly this morning," Jess added, referring to the other two detectives on their team, Mack Grey and Noah Wilder. "We agreed that if any of us heard anything, we'd tell the other two right away."

And Liam had a lot to fill them in on. He glanced down at the truck, now with altered plates, he'd parked in the alley below. "I've got people with me. A friend of mine and a baby. My..." He swallowed hard and forced the words over his lips. "My granddaughter. Turns out I have a baby granddaughter. They need a place to hide."

Jess's blue eyes went wide.

But all she said was "Well, they're safe here. I've still got one of Dominic's old cribs and playpens here. I'm pretty sure we have formula. There are a few diapers in the bathroom. I don't know if we'd have any the baby's size, but we might. Check in the back of the cupboard. Either way, there's a drugstore just down the street."

Travis had become like a father figure to little Willow and Dominic while in witness protection and he'd eventually adopted them when they became orphaned. The love that Jess felt for Travis and the kids practically radiated through her. Gratitude overwhelmed him.

"Thank you," he said. "But we can't stay."

"Of course you can stay." Jess's arms crossed.

"But, it's your wedding day," Liam said.

"Yeah, I know it's my wedding day." She laughed. "I'm the one in the big white dress. And you're not going to miss it. How many years have we worked together? Five? Six? And how many times did you save my life or have my back?"

He wasn't sure. He didn't keep count. It wasn't the kind of thing a person did in a job like this.

"Travis, the kids and I might not even be alive today without your backup," Jess said. "So you're coming to my wedding and that's final. The church has a small balcony that's never used. We'll close it off and you can hide there. We'll find somebody both you and I trust to watch the baby. Then after the wedding, we'll sit down with the rest of the team and figure this all out."

He almost laughed. "But. It's. Your. Wedding. Day."

"I know!" She laughed. "And don't worry. I'm heading to church soon and getting married in about an hour. I'll still catch a flight to Florida with my new husband for our honeymoon tonight. Noah and Holly will still be getting married tomorrow and Mack and Iris will still be getting married on New Year's Eve. But we can still be there for you, too."

Jess's smile was gentle, but her blue eyes were strong.

"Go get your friend and your granddaughter," Jess insisted. "We'll get them sorted, and I'll fill the team in. Just let me have the wedding and get married, then we'll carve out a little bit of time to meet back here and hash things out before the reception. It'll give Travis and I a nice little interlude between doing all the fancy, formal wedding things. Considering the fact we have a one-year-old and a six-year-old in the wedding party, we planned a pretty short ceremony, and the reception's a potluck at the volunteer fire hall." Her eyes glanced to the clock. "I should have the team back here in two and a half hours. Maybe three. Don't worry. It'll be fine."

"Thank you," Liam said, suddenly finding it hard to speak words as something welled in his throat.

Sure, he'd been there to help rescue her, Travis and the children from violent criminals, and to assist her out of a few tight spots. But that was the job. That was what he did. Maybe even, on some level, what

God had put him on the planet to do. What Jess was doing now somehow felt like so much more.

"Now again, hurry up and get your people," Jess said. "I can't wait to meet them."

His people. Huh. He'd never thought of himself as having people before.

"Kelly," he said. "My friend's name is Kelly. She's…the grandmother of my grandchild. We haven't seen each other in a very long time. I didn't even know we had a child. The baby's name is Pip. It's a nickname. They haven't named her yet." He ran his hand over the back of his neck. "Sorry, I don't even know what to say about this situation yet. It's all very complicated and confusing."

Jess nodded. "Family often is."

And there was something about the simplicity of her answer that helped.

"Not sure how to say this, but you look really nice, by the way," Liam added, partly to change the subject, but mostly because it was true. "Like a princess only not cheesy."

"Thank you," Jess said. "Willow helped pick it out. She has a matching dress in navy and silver. According to Travis, she was running around in the cape all last night and he barely talked her out of sleeping in it. Considering she's six, my getup could've been much more sparkly. I barely talked her out of tiaras."

Liam chuckled. "Travis was really blessed to find you."

"We're blessed to have found each other."

Liam turned to go, then paused as a question he'd forgotten to ask crossed his mind. "Why do you have your service weapon—a gun—in your wedding dress?"

"Because for some reason the world thinks Liam Bearsmith is dead," Jess said. "And while I didn't know why or what that meant, I was pretty sure he couldn't be."

He could still hear her laughing as he

climbed back down the fire escape to get Kelly and Pip, and then he hid the truck.

There was something peaceful, almost homelike, about how the next hour passed. Jess let them in through the closed bookstore instead of making them climb the fire escape with the baby. It turned out there was indeed a diaper Pip's size hiding in the back of the closet, and before Jess left to join her bridesmaids and get ready for her wedding, she had a friend drop by with a fresh box of diapers, two different types of formula and a bag of donated baby clothes. Then Liam and Kelly camped out on the living-room floor and spread out a Noah's Arc play mat for Pip to stretch and wriggle on, along with fuzzy animal toys that squeaked, crinkled and rattled. They leaned against pillows, played with the baby and ate a simple meal of ham-and-cheese sandwiches and fruit, thanks to Jess's insistence they help clear out what was left in the fridge.

A small television was on in the corner and they watched the twenty-four-hour news station, with the sound off, for news about the Imposters. Kelly's phone charged and Liam used one of Travis's tablet computers to scan the internet in vain for more information about the new Imposters, Hannah's kidnapping and his supposed death.

Despite the tension and fear, a comfortable silence fell between them, while hundreds of words tumbled silently through Liam's brain that he left unsaid. He glanced over to where Kelly was kneeling, her long dark hair falling around her face as she played with Pip.

Something ached like a deep wound buried by scar tissue inside his chest.

Lord, I'd have given anything for this beautiful, amazing woman to be my family. Why were we torn apart? Who can we be to each other now?

She glanced up, as if sensing his gaze. Their eyes met. Emotions crashed like waves over his heart.

I wish I hadn't believed you'd moved on without me. I wish I'd been brave enough to show up at your door and find out myself. I wish I hadn't let my father talk me into forgetting you and moving on, for the sake of my career. I wish I'd had the courage to have my heart broken to my face. I should've come back for you.

Her lips parted slowly. He watched as silent words formed there. But before she could speak them, a buzz sounded behind her. She spun.

"It's the phone!" she yelped. She snatched it from the cord. "It's Renner. I've got a message from Renner!"

She squeezed the phone in both hands for a moment and clutched it to her chest. Then she typed a quick response and set it back down.

"It's all good news," she said. "Renner has found Hannah. He'll be rescuing her later today and then coming to pick up Pip and I. We'll all be reunited and leaving Canada by tonight."

The warmth and joy that flushed her cheeks did nothing to temper the cold dread that spread over Liam's limbs. Something about this was wrong. Very wrong. But for once his mind was too murky to figure out what.

Then she frowned. "Renner's telling me to turn on the news."

He turned to the television and froze as he stared in disbelief at the face filling the screen.

"A warrant has been issued for hacker Seth Miles's arrest," he said, reading out loud, "on suspicion of being the Imposter mastermind behind the holiday party boat hijacking."

NINE

"Don't believe it!" Liam said quickly. "Just because the news says that Seth's an Imposter doesn't make it true. I don't know why the news is saying that, but there has to be a reason."

"The Imposters are exactly the kind of group he'd have teamed up with in the past," Kelly said.

"I know," Liam said. "But he's changed."

Footsteps sounded on the stairs.

"Get behind me!" he ordered. In an instant, he leaped in front of Pip and Kelly, sheltering them with his body, just as two figures appeared at the top of the stairs.

Tall and lanky, Detective Mack Grey had an intensity that had allowed him to move through countless criminal hotbeds undetected, while his fiancée, social worker Iris James, had a light and airy smile that lit up a room, which was coupled with an endless drive to help those in need. They'd fallen in love when Mack had been undercover and he'd risked everything to be with Iris. And yet, it was nothing compared to what Liam would've faced if his relationship with Kelly had become public.

Notably, despite the fact that Jess's wedding was probably minutes away, they were both in blue jeans and sweatshirts.

"Whoa, hey! What are you guys doing here?" Tension fled Liam's shoulders as he stepped sideways and reached for Kelly's hand to help her up. "Kelly, this is Mack, one of the detectives on my team, and Iris, who runs a homeless drop-in center in downtown Toronto. Two of the best people I know."

"Nice to meet you!" Kelly said, and as she stepped beside him, Liam found himself brushing Kelly's back right between her shoulder blades. Her hand reached out and shook theirs in turn. Then she glanced down. "This is Pip."

Liam gestured to the television screen. "Tell me you know something about this."

"Yeah." Mack nodded. "A friend gave me a heads-up about the warrant. I don't know where they're getting the intel and I don't believe it for a moment." Then the detective looked down at Pip. Liam watched as a question hovered in Mack's eyes. He suspected his colleague had heard the rumor and wanted to hear from Liam's own mouth if it was true. "Now, please tell me this isn't what I think it is."

"Pip is...her... My... Our...granddaughter," Liam said. As awkward as the words felt leaving his lips, somehow they felt just a little bit easier every time he said them. "Kelly and I met a very long time ago, when I was placing her in witness protection. She's the hacker who kept Hannah Phillips's file out of the Imposters's hands last year. Hannah is our daughter... I—I didn't know about Hannah or Pip until yesterday."

Mack didn't say anything at first. Instead, he just stood there, his eyes on Liam's face. It was like two gunslingers waiting to see if the other would flinch as an uncomfortable pause spread around the room.

"Mack tried to place me in witness protection, too," Iris said to Kelly, as the two women sat on the play mat and turned their attention to Pip.

But there was far more to the story than that. And Liam understood, or at least he thought he did, the conflicting emotions behind Mack's gaze.

Mack had been suspended and had faced a significant knock to his career after it was suspected he and Iris had gotten too close when he was on an undercover assignment. This was despite the fact Mack had never even acted on his romantic attraction to Iris. Mack had risked absolutely everything for the woman he was about to marry. He'd paid a hefty price for falling in love on assignment. But Liam had broken the rules on a much bigger scale, kept it pretty much a secret and then had gone on to have a stellar career afterward with people being none the wiser.

"I didn't know," Liam told Mack quietly, stepping away from the women and lowering his voice. "Someone covered it up. I'm guessing to protect me. I was immediately sent on a long undercover assignment. None of Kelly's messages got to me and her RCMP witness-protection file was doctored. I will always regret I didn't do more to fight for her back then."

It was an admission that had been building for a long time, like steam wanting to escape from the top of his heart. And considering everything Mack had been through to be with Iris, he was the right person to admit it to.

"But what happens now?" Mack asked. "If word gets out that you fathered a child with a witness—even if it was twenty years ago—there will be consequences. You'll be investigated. You could be suspended or demoted. You might even be fired."

Or nobody ever has to know. Liam felt something inside him push back. Kelly was still planning on leaving the country with Hannah, Renner and Pip. He'd only confided anything about the relationship to a tiny handful of people, all of whom he trusted. There was no reason why the news would need to come out. Not unless Kelly wanted to stay in his life in some kind of present and visible way, and there was no proof or evidence she wanted to do that.

"In case you haven't heard, I'm dead," Liam said with a laugh that even sounded hollow to himself.

"So you'd actually keep it a secret?" Mack asked, and again, there was an edge to his voice. No, it was more like a knife, peeling away at something Liam didn't want touched. And even though he knew

Mack was a good man who meant well and wanted what was best for him, Liam felt his jaw tighten.

"Don't worry," Liam said. "I'll do the right thing." *As soon as I figure out what that is and where we go from here.* "Shouldn't you be heading to the wedding?"

"We're actually here to babysit," Mack said, raising his voice to include Kelly and Iris, as well. "We're going to watch Pip for an hour while you and Kelly go to the wedding. Jess said she's got the balcony closed off, so you guys can sit there."

Liam watched as his friend's arms crossed over his strong chest. His tone, while warm, implied it wasn't up for debate. No wonder they'd both shown up in jeans.

"You should go to the wedding," Liam stated.

"And so should you," Mack countered. "You've worked with Jess even more than I have. Iris and I don't even know

Travis. Jess and Travis wouldn't even be getting married if you hadn't helped save their lives." Then he glanced at Iris and something softened in his eyes. "Iris and I wouldn't be getting married on New Year's Eve if you hadn't helped save our lives, either. Liam, we owe our lives to you. I know I do."

Liam's head shook. "I'm not going to let you——"

"Stop." Mack held up a hand. "Let me do this. You've done so very much for me. For all of us. Besides, it'll give me a chance to just hang out with Iris and relax. Between everything going on at the drop-in center over Christmas, two weddings this weekend and our own wedding next week, we haven't had a quiet hour to just sit around and do nothing in forever. I can also use the time to read up on your so-called death, the warrant out against Seth, the Imposters and Hannah and Renner Phillips for when we all meet up and plan our way forward between the wedding and reception." Then he grinned. "And we'll still be going to the reception. I'm not missing barbecued ribs and cake."

Liam chuckled softly. If he stood here and argued with Mack much longer, none of them would be making it to the wedding. Besides, Mack was already sitting on the play mat.

"I give you my word your granddaughter will be safe," Mack said. "I will guard her with my life."

Liam knew he would. He turned to Kelly and as she started to stand, he found himself reaching for her hand.

"What do you think?" he asked as her fingers lingered for a moment in his. "Mack is an incredible officer, and I'd trust him with my life and yours and Pip's. The church is only a few minutes' walk from here. But I'm not going anywhere without you. I want to be there if Renner calls or if you get an update on Hannah. Whatever we decide, I think we should stick together."

He didn't know how to explain it to her, let alone to himself, but something inside him couldn't bear the thought of not having Kelly there by his side.

Kelly looked up at him and bit her lip. And he realized she still hadn't pulled her hand away from his.

"Pip will be safe here," he added. "Travis installed a state-of-the-art security system in this apartment when he was first placed in witness protection, and then Seth upgraded it even more."

He felt himself frown as he said Seth's name. Where was he? Why had he decided to skip Jess and Travis's wedding? Why was the world now convinced he was an Imposter? True, Seth had made some dubious decisions. But still.

"Iris runs both teen-mom and high-risk parenting groups at the drop-in," Mack added. Pride gleamed in his eyes as he looked at his fiancée. "I promise you we'll keep Pip safe."

"But it's up to you," Liam said. "If you want to stay, we stay."

"And where I go, you go," Kelly said, softly. She nodded slightly, as if coming to a decision, then pulled her hand from his and turned to Mack. "Thank you. I don't know how much Pip is able to pick up of what we're feeling. But maybe it will be good for Pip to have a break from us to play with a friendly new face. I think I need to take a walk, breathe and pray, too. And right now a church feels like the right place to be."

Yeah, he understood that feeling, too. Pip cooed and waved her arms at him as Liam bent down to kiss the top of the tiny baby's head goodbye. He was surprised just how much it tugged at his heartstrings to leave her, even if it was only for an hour and with someone he trusted implicitly. How hard would it be when Kelly and Pip left his life for good?

Kelly declined Iris's kind offer to lend her something fancy, but accepted her follow-up offer of a spare T-shirt and change of sweater. She'd freshened up and done something else to her appearance before they left, too, but Liam wasn't sure what. Changed her hair, maybe? Added lip gloss? He wasn't sure. All he knew as they walked in comfortable silence to the small church was that Kelly somehow looked even more beautiful than ever in a way he couldn't put a finger on.

The small church sat alone on a small rural road surrounded by fields. It was already full—the service was about to start and nobody seemed to notice them—as they snuck in a side door and up into the empty balcony. There they sat, on battered folding chairs, and watched as the wedding unfolded beneath them. Travis stood at the front of the church, holding baby Dominic in his arms—they wore matching tuxedos with dark blue bow ties. Willow practically twirled with joy as she walked Jess down the aisle, their smiles shining more than the dazzling beads on their dresses and the winter light shimmering through the window ever could.

Liam felt Kelly's thumb run over his and he looked down at their hands. Their fingers were linked. And he couldn't even remember when they'd started holding hands or which one of them had initiated it.

Noah Wilder, the fourth and final detective on his team, and his fiancée, Corporal Holly Asher, stepped up to the lectern and began to read a passage from Song of Solomon together. "'Set me as a seal upon thine heart, as a seal upon thine arm, for love is strong as death...'"

"They're the couple getting married tomorrow," Liam whispered. "They're also the two that stopped the witness-protection auction and were there when the initial Imposters were killed. If these Imposters are out for revenge, these two are probably in the line of fire, too."

Kelly nodded.

"'Many waters cannot quench love, neither can the floods drown it,'" Noah and Holly continued. "'If a man would give all the substance of his house for love, it would be utterly contemned.'"

Contemned, Liam thought. In other words, it was contemptible to trade worldly possessions for love. And what had he traded for love? A career? A job? His father had spent his childhood drilling into him that close relationships and a career taking out bad guys just didn't mix. But during the past year, Liam had watched the other three detectives on his team, and the people they were now marrying, give up so much for each other. And Liam hadn't even been willing to drive to Kelly's door and see for himself that she'd moved on for someone else.

"Have you ever wished for all that?" Kelly whispered. "A marriage, a family, kids?"

"Never," Liam admitted. "Not even once. To be honest, once I was told you'd moved on without me, and we disappeared from each other's lives, the thought of marriage and kids never crossed my mind again."

"Because of your job?" she asked.

"Because of you," Liam said. "Because losing you hurt so much I didn't even know if my stupid broken heart was even capable of beating again."

He watched as her lips parted, then he looked down at their hands.

"I've been shot," he said. "Too many times. I've been stabbed, punched and kicked. My nose has been broken. I've had a concussion and been in a medically induced coma. I've faced down way too many rooms full of killers. And somehow, none of that ever scared me off going right back into another undercover case. I never even hesitated. I guess I was just wired that way."

Then he pulled his hand away from hers, feeling their fingers brush against each other as they parted.

"But losing you was a one-and-done

thing for me," he admitted. "It was the worst thing I'd ever gone through and I never wanted to feel it again."

Everyone stood and the room burst into song. The service was ending. He touched Kelly's arm, guiding her to follow him as he dropped to the floor so that anyone looking up while leaving wouldn't spot them. She sat cross-legged and he sat with his back to the wedding, facing her.

"I told myself and anyone else who would listen that I was married to my job," Liam said. "But maybe, if I'm honest, it was always you."

"It was always you for me, too," she said.

Below them he could hear people shuffling out of the church. Kelly leaned forward and her hand brushed his jaw. He couldn't imagine ever trusting anyone else to touch his face like that. His fingers ran up into her hair.

Then he kissed her. Despite the fact he was still in no place for a relationship, their lives were uncertain and she'd be leaving his life as soon as Renner texted her back, he let his lips linger on hers and his hand reach for hers. Here alone in the church balcony, surrounded by the smells of wood and candles, old books and flowers, it was just him and Kelly. And he wasn't about to miss what could be his last chance to hold her the way his foolish heart had longed to since he'd first laid eyes on her back on the docks.

They broke the kiss, but didn't pull away. Instead they stayed there, with Kelly's head on Liam's shoulder and his arms around her as they listened to the final person leave, and then the lights switched off. Only then did they both end the hug and stand. They walked down the staircase in silence, as if both their hearts were heavy with words neither of them knew how to speak, then stepped out the side door, into the cold. The door clicked shut behind them. Pale, barren fields covered in snow spread out ahead of them.

"Ready to head back to the apartment, meet up with my team and plan our way out of this?" Liam asked.

But before Kelly could answer, he heard the sound of someone running. Instinctively, Liam turned back toward the church. Kelly's hand was already on the handle of the door they'd just gone through. Her eyes met his. "It's locked!"

"Liam!" A figure dashed around the corner. And Liam blinked. It was Seth. The hacker's form was swamped in a puffy, hooded coat, and a ski hat was pulled down over his shaggy head.

"Seth!" Liam said. "Hey, what are you doing here? Why does the television think you're an Imposter?"

"Long story." Seth was panting so hard he had to bend over to catch his breath. "I've got a car. It's parked down the street. You guys have to come with me. Now."

"No!" Kelly said, saying the word before Liam could. "We've got to go back to the apartment and get Pip."

"You can't." Seth shook his head. His eyes were pained and he was still gasping for breath. "You've got to come with me. Now. No time to explain."

"Why?" Liam asked. He reached out and put a hand on Seth's shoulder. The hacker flinched under the touch. "Stop, take a deep breath, calm down and tell me what's going on."

"I'm not going anywhere with you," Kelly said. Her arms crossed. "Not without a real good explanation."

He heard the cars before he saw them, two expensive-looking black sedans—they pulled up on either side, blocking them in. Armed and masked men stepped out of both sides, wearing not only the same black Imposter masks, but also, incongruously, the same colored eye patches they had when taking people hostage on the boat. Kelly's hand grabbed his. The door was locked, their backs were against the wall, they were outnumbered and surrounded on both sides. There was nothing for Kelly to hide behind. Not this time. If shooting broke out there was no way to keep her out of the line of fire.

Help me, Lord! What do I do? How do I get her out of here safely?

But it was the look of guilt in Seth's eyes that scared him most of all.

"Liam, I'm sorry," Seth gasped. "They—they were waiting in the alley beside the bookstore."

Horror rose up inside Liam. "What did you do?"

Then as he watched, Seth turned and faced the masked men.

"Well, I did it!" Seth called, almost theatrically, despite the fact he was still rasping from being out of breath. "I led you to them. Now where's my money? I told you, if you want the credit for this one, I'm not letting you have it for free."

"You led them to us?" Anger radiated through Kelly's voice as it rose to a hiss and Liam suspected that despite being surrounded by weapons, it was only the slight pressure of Liam's own hand on her wrist that kept her from lunging at Seth.

"Yeah, let's go with that." Seth stepped forward, glancing at the masked men flanking them on either side. His chin rose. "No hard feelings, but you know I was never a true part of your team. You never respected me like you did the others or let me forget my past. And now with everyone going off to their own thing, what was going to happen to me? I'm just supposed to go back to a life of witness protection? I had nothing before I joined your team. Law enforcement had even banned me from using a computer or going online, until you and your buddies came along and convinced me to help you solve crime."

Liam remembered all too well. Seth's life had been not much more than glorified house arrest when they'd invited him to join their team. And while his heart told him there was no way Seth would betray them and there had to be a good explanation for everything, he could still hear the tremor of truth moving through Seth's words.

"Besides," Seth added, "these guys pooled together and are offering me ten thousand dollars for letting them get the credit and video footage of your kidnapping. I mean, what's the point of a mob if people aren't vying to climb over others to rise to the top?" Seth raised his cell phone and aimed it at the masked men and away from Liam and Kelly. "Chop, chop. Hurry up. Otherwise I'll stream this whole conversation on the dark web, and everyone will know you not only bribed me to get credit for my hostages, you don't pay your debts."

For a moment, nobody moved. Then a masked man with a green eye patch tapped some buttons on his phone and Seth's phone beeped. The hacker glanced at his screen and grinned like someone had painted a smile on his pale face. *What are you doing, Seth? What is the game plan?* Liam could feel Kelly's pulse racing under his fingertips. *Was I wrong to trust him?*

"Congratulations, gentlemen," the hacker said. "Now everyone will know you mean business."

The Imposters moved in toward them on either side.

"I mean, sure, I've got a pretty big target on my head, too." Seth leaned forward and clasped Liam in an awkward hug as if wishing him luck. "But I've disappeared before. I can do it again. I'm just sorry you're going to miss your candlelight vigil."

Then Kelly screamed in fury as masked Imposters yanked her from his grasp.

Imposters gagged her mouth and handcuffed her hands behind her back, then picked her up and tossed her into the huge trunk of one of the black and very expensive-looking cars. Her heart pounded in her chest. Panic welled up inside her, sending hot tears to the corners of her eyes. Then she heard the sounds of a struggle and saw the light disappear as Liam's handcuffed body tumbled in beside her. The trunk slammed shut with a bang that seemed to shake the darkness around them. She felt the sound of the engine rumbling beneath them and cold air seeping in as the car began to drive. The fabric of the gag tasted stale in her mouth. The sickly smell of a freshly shampooed car interior filled her nostrils. Then she felt Liam's strong form roll beside her. She leaned into him and, slowly, felt the warmth of his core. He couldn't speak, he couldn't hold her and she couldn't see his face in the darkness. And yet something about just knowing he was there seemed to push back against the panic threatening to overtake her.

The road grew bumpy beneath them. The trunk rattled, rumbled and jolted. Liam rolled away from her and for a moment, she was all alone in the darkness.

Then she heard him roll back, his legs bumped hers and she felt his breath on her face.

"Don't worry," he said softly and she wondered how Liam had freed his mouth from the gag. "Pip will be okay. No matter what's going on with Seth, I guarantee Mack and Iris won't let anything happen to her. With what's on the news, Mack won't even let Seth near her. He's the most protective man I know."

Fear pounded through her heart. How could he possibly know that? She'd told him that she didn't trust Seth. He'd argued with her that the hacker should be trusted. And look where it had gotten her? Bound. Gagged. Tossed into the trunk of a car. Kidnapped by the same criminals who'd kidnapped her daughter, Hannah. She just prayed that Renner had managed to rescue Hannah and that someone would find them.

"Hey," Liam said softly. "It's okay. It's all going to be okay. I promise."

And she wondered if he could somehow feel or sense her racing heartbeat.

"Now, I need you to stay as still as you can," Liam said. "I'm going to get your gag off and it might hurt a little bit. Now, don't move. I'm fairly hopeful this will work."

She felt him lean closer, his mouth brushed just behind her ear, a shiver ran through her skin and then she felt a swift tug as the fabric tore. For a brief instant pain shot though her skull, then it stopped as she felt the gag fall from her face.

She gasped a breath, thankful to feel air fill her lungs. "How did you get the gag off?"

"My gag?" Liam asked. "Old trick. Clench your jaw when they put it on, then relax it when you're alone. Gives you a tiny bit of wiggle room. Then use the friction of your shoulder to ease it off your mouth. Like I said, I've been doing this job a really long time."

Okay, but while this might not be the

first time he'd been bound, gagged and thrown into the trunk of a car, something in his tone implied a silent *but* hovering in the darkness.

"Then how did you get mine off?" she asked, suspecting she knew the answer.

"Tore it off," Liam said. "Well, bit and ripped. Just behind your ear so as not to hurt your face. You can rip most fabrics off your wrists that way if you know how to tear against the grain."

"Including gags?" she asked.

"Apparently," Liam said. "That was a first for me. Everything is a first with you."

For a moment they lay there side by side in the darkness.

"I haven't quite figured out how to get my arms free yet," he admitted. "With rope, fabric, duct tape or even zip ties, your best option is to find something sharp to tear them off with. Although sometimes it takes a long time, it's doable eventually.

But handcuffs are trickier. Have you got anything in your pocket?"

"No, I don't," she said and rolled from side to side to double-check. "Actually, no wait. I still have my burner cell."

Even in the darkness she could tell that Liam jolted.

"They didn't take it?" he asked.

"They patted me down quickly," she said. "But the phone's tucked inside my jacket and I guess they didn't feel it or find it."

"Mmm-hmm." Liam made a noncommittal sound. "That's an interesting mistake for them to make."

"You think they did it on purpose?" she asked.

"I think, I don't know," Liam said. "Maybe. Clearly they're after Renner. Maybe they're hoping he'll call and they can use you as bait. But it's also likely the person who patted you down was an amateur who'd never kidnapped anyone before. These new Imposters are basically an online mob, following whatever loud idea floats to the top of their message board."

"And maybe Seth's one of them," Kelly countered.

"I doubt it," Liam said.

"Then why did he lead them to us?" she demanded.

"I don't know," Liam said.

"The news said he was the head of the Imposters." She could hear the bitter and angry bite in her voice and didn't try to hide it. "And don't tell me the Imposters are a swarm without a leader, because those men clearly thought he was on their side. They didn't shoot him or kidnap him. They bribed him. Why do you think that is?"

"I don't know," Liam said again. His voice was oddly neutral in the darkness. She didn't need neutral. Not now. She needed anger, or reassurance, or something. She needed emotion. "I don't know what to think."

"How can you not know what to think?" Her voice rose.

"I don't have enough information!" Liam's voice rose, too, but not like he was upset at her, more like he was trapped. "I don't know why Seth did what he did. I know that he used to hack bad guys. He'd convinced himself he was doing the right thing and that the only way to do that was off-the-grid. He didn't trust law enforcement. For a long time, Seth didn't know if he could trust me. We bumped heads over his methods more times that I could count and our personalities never really clicked. But…" His voice trailed off and for a long moment he didn't say anything. "But…oh, wow, I just realized he hugged me goodbye."

"So?" Kelly asked.

"So neither Seth or I are huggy people," Liam said. "Seth is the last person I'd expect to hug me like that. If I roll over, can you check my jacket? He might've slipped something in my pocket."

"Sure," she said, even though it sounded like he was grasping at straws. But they shuffled and jostled, turning this way and that in the shaking trunk, until finally her fingers brushed his jacket pocket.

"Do you feel anything?" he asked.

"Not yet," she said. She felt around the corner of his pocket, then her fingers brushed something thin and plastic. "Wait, yes." She pulled it out. "I think it's a twist tie. You know, the kind you use to close a bag of bread?"

Liam let out a long breath. "Okay, we got something. Let me take it from you and I'll go to work."

She felt him pry it from her fingertips and roll away.

"You think Seth slipped a twist tie into your jacket pocket?" she asked. "Because he knew you could use it to pick handcuffs that are behind your back?"

"I don't know," Liam said again. "But I'm going to get your handcuffs off first. Now, please, lie as still as you can."

She did as he asked. His fingers moved against hers for a while, then there was a clink and her handcuffs fell from her wrists. *Thank You, God!*

"Thank you," she said. Her freed arms hugged his shoulders quickly. Then she pulled out her phone. No cell signal. "But I don't know how to do the same for you."

"It's okay." Liam let out a long and weary breath. "I can do it. I just need to get my hands in front of me. Which if I was twenty years younger would be as simple as sliding my legs through my arms almost like a somersault. As it is, I'm going to have to dislocate my shoulder."

She gasped.

"You don't happen to remember how to put my shoulder back in its socket?" he asked.

He'd dislocated it two decades ago while fighting for their lives when they'd been under attack from the men sent to kidnap her. They'd escaped together with her driving getaway and Liam's shoulder still out of its socket. Then he'd talked her through popping it back in for him when they'd been safe and alone. It had been pretty emotionally intense for her, seeing how much pain he'd been in.

It had been the first time they'd kissed.

"I think I remember," she said. "If not, I'm sure you can talk me through it."

She hated the thought of him being in that much pain again. But what choice did they have? They were still locked in a trunk, the car was still speeding somewhere to their unknown destination and they had no way to contact the outside world. She gave Liam's shoulders another quick hug. Then she waited in the darkness and prayed, as she heard a pained shout leave Liam's throat as he wrenched his shoulder from its socket and then maneuvered his hands around in front of him. Then carefully, deliberately and at his direction, she helped him pop his shoulder back into place.

"It's going to be okay." Liam's voice

was ragged as he picked his own hand-
cuffs, aided by the light of her cell phone.
She couldn't imagine the pain he was in.
"Sometimes you've got to go old school.
And this is pretty much as old school as
it gets."

The handcuffs clinked.

"You get them open?" she asked.

But before Liam could answer, she felt
the world yanked out from under her, as
she found herself tossed hard against the
hood of the trunk. Pain shot through her
body. Then the world around her flipped
again, gravity suddenly losing all mean-
ing as she felt her body fly into the back
of the trunk. The car was flipping, end
over end, flying out of control.

They were crashing.

TEN

The car was rolling and tumbling down an incline. How steep was the hill? How long would they fall? What would they hit at the bottom? She didn't know. For a moment, all she could do was shield her head and pray as she was violently tossed around, terrified. Then she felt Liam throw his arms around her and clutch her to his chest, cradling her with his body, praying over her and keeping her safe, as they fell together into the darkness.

Then, just as suddenly as it had started, the vehicle stopped rolling with a jolt and everything went still. Odd shapes of light seeped through the edges of the bent and smashed trunk hood, and it took her a moment to realize the car was upright again.

"Still alive?" Liam asked, his voice low and deep in her ear.

"Yeah."

"Injured?"

"No..."

"Hurt?" he persisted, and she almost smiled.

"Probably," she said. "But nothing major."

"Thank You, God," he said. Then slowly he let her go, easing her from his arms as carefully and gently as if she was made of glass. Then he began to kick hard with both legs, repeatedly and rhythmically stomping against the dented trunk hood until it flew open. Winter sunlight streamed in.

"One second," he said. He climbed out and disappeared from view. Moments later he was back. He reached in for her hands—she let him take them and leaped out into knee-deep snow.

"It's just us," he said. "They're gone. I'm guessing they bailed out when the car spun out of control."

Blue sky stretched above snow-capped trees. A long steep hill was to her right, picturesque in unbroken snow, except for the harsh slashes, littered with broken glass and bumpers, where the car had tumbled down it. A road was empty above them. Then, finally, she steeled herself to look at the car they'd just escaped. It was a flattened wreck, like a child's toy that someone had stomped on.

"By the looks of things, the computer went haywire," Liam added. "If I had to guess, somebody hacked the car's computer. I've seen Seth do it before. But I don't know if it was him. Or if whoever did it was trying to kill them or rescue us. All I know is they're gone and we're alone. This apparently wasn't planned because nobody stuck around to film it."

A quick scan of the vehicle found nothing worth taking. They trudged up the hill, following the path of destruction.

"Yeah, yeah, I know shouting 'Detective Liam Bearsmith, RCMP' isn't going to be much help right now," he said as they reached the road, and an unexpected giggle burst through her lips, thankfully breaking the tension in her chest. "But old-school detective work, like looking at tire tracks and footprints, tells me the car swerved out of control here." He pointed at a mess of tire tracks. "The driver didn't even have the opportunity to try and regain control. He and his passengers just leaped out...there." He followed the path of their footprints. "A second car was traveling so close behind the first it had to swerve to avoid it. They all hopped in the back seat, turned around and kept driving. If I had to guess, none of them saw this coming, and when they saw how the car crashed they assumed we were dead. Again..."

His words trailed off as his hands rose in frustration.

"We're dealing with a mob, not an organized group," she concluded. "Setting aside for one moment whatever's going on with Seth."

"Right," Liam said. "Don't ask me how we take them down, because I don't know. They're too big and unwieldy. We'd have to not only shut down the entire Imposters online operation, but track every single person who logged into their site. And who knows how many people that is? We'd need not only an entire online team, but then a full-scale operation to coordinate people on the ground to find and arrest these people." Liam glanced back down the hill at the wrecked car and shook his head. "Gotta say, two presumed deaths in twenty-four hours is a couple more than I'm used to."

Kelly patted his arm. "Welcome to the club."

He chuckled. "Well," he said, "we're alive and we've got Renner's phone, a twist tie and each other."

"I think this is where you tell me that you've survived worse," she said.

"I have," he agreed. "And with much worse company."

His hands slid onto her shoulders and she stepped toward his chest, and as she tilted her face up to look at him he bent his down toward hers. Their lips almost met. But this time neither of them seemed willing to move that extra inch. She wasn't quite sure why. But something inside her was holding her back and it seemed to be holding him back, too.

"So what do we do now?" she asked.

Liam's features set into a picture of determination. He stepped back and as their bodies parted, he crossed his arms over his chest.

"All right," he said. "For now, we walk. We'll follow the road and wherever possible head south because that's usually the fastest way to find civilization in Ontario. I'm guessing there's still no message from Renner, and the fact that Seth asked you not to use the phone is now giving me a weird feeling about it. We need allies, we need answers and Seth's comment about attending my own memorial vigil keeps rattling around in my head. Judging by the sky, it's somewhere between two and three. The candlelight vigil is in Ottawa, which is four hours from where the wedding was in Kilpatrick, and happens at seven. That gives us about five hours to figure out where we are and get there." He sighed. "Old-school detective work takes a whole lot of thinking."

"Or hopefully," she said, "Renner will call any moment to let us know Hannah is safe, he'll come pick us up and we'll go get Pip."

But her phone stayed stubbornly quiet as the afternoon spread out long, slow and empty, like all the afternoons they'd spent together back when they'd been on the run. They walked for over forty minutes and turned down several hitchhiking offers from people Liam apparently didn't like the look of before Liam accepted a ride from a young man, who looked to be barely more than a teenager, with a beat-up car that had a car seat in the back that smelled like it had recently been wiped down with sanitizing wipes. Liam sat in the front, where he and the driver made small talk about the weather and didn't exchange names. Then, when he dropped them off in a small town, Liam slipped him fifty dollars.

"Why him?" Kelly asked as he drove away.

"That's a good kid with a criminal record, consisting of a minor offence or two," Liam said, nodding at the departing car. "My hunch is minor drug possession or drunk driving. He's no longer with his baby's mother but is trying to do right by his kid. Didn't get many breaks in life and doesn't want trouble. Just wants to keep his head down."

"You got all that from a quick glance?" Kelly asked.

"Yup." Liam nodded. "My old-school

skills haven't gotten totally rusty. Like I said, I've survived this job a long time."

He led them past both a coffee shop and a restaurant before they finally stopped at a diner that had a pay phone out front. It took buying a map from a nearby gas station to get correct change. But Liam finally had it and they stood outside in the snow while he stared at the phone as if trying to decide what number to call. Then he punched in a number and stood back. The phone rang. It clicked through to the answering machine and then a few bars of "Be My Baby" by the Ronettes played, followed immediately by a couple of lines from an even older song from Bobby Darin about a shark's pearly teeth.

Liam hung up and his hand shook as he set the receiver back. "Thank You, God."

Her hand brushed his back. "'Mack the Knife'?" she asked. "What does that mean?"

He turned toward her, relief filling his

eyes. "It means Mack and Iris still have Pip and she's safe."

And suddenly it hit her. He'd been even more worried about Pip's safety than she'd been. Because when he'd promised her that Pip was safe, she'd believed him.

"Who did you call?" she asked.

"A very long time ago, when I was training to be a cop, I was friends with a guy named Trent," Liam explained. "An excellent cop, now an RCMP detective, who went on to marry an exceptional OPP detective named Chloe. Back when we were teenagers, cell phones weren't that big a thing, or if they were we couldn't afford them, so we'd call each other's answering machines directly and leave messages. Trent and I agreed to keep one open as an emergency messaging device. It's the closest thing we could get to an untraceable number. An unused twenty-five-year-old phone number is the last thing anyone's going to be tapping. Like me, Trent used to go undercover in a lot of very rough assignments, sometimes for months at a time with really bad people."

"Very old school," Kelly said. "How many times have you used the number?"

"In over twentysomething years?" Liam asked. "He's used it maybe twice."

"And you?" she asked.

"This is the first time I've called it," Liam said, and there was a weight to his words she didn't quite understand.

"How did he even know you'd call that number?" she asked.

"He didn't." They kept walking. "He probably followed a hunch and took a shot in the dark because he heard something from someone he trusts. It was an act of faith and hope."

"So these new Imposters aren't the only ones with a network," she said. "You seem to have a lot of people looking out for you, wanting to help you."

He didn't look at her. He just kept walking. "Cops look out for each other."

"Jess offered to help you on her wedding

day," she countered. "Mack and Iris are taking care of Pip. An old buddy called a secret number you set up over twenty years ago. That's way more than cops looking out for each other."

He didn't answer and she wasn't sure why. It was like there was something inside Liam blocking him from seeing how much he mattered to people. Just like he apparently hadn't seen just how much he'd mattered to her.

"Come on," he said. "We should eat something and figure out our next ride."

They reached a diner and Liam scanned it for lines of sight. Their conversation dropped to low and innocuous small talk, as they went inside, hid in a corner booth and bought greasy burgers that they paid cash for. A television mounted in the corner ran the twenty-four-hour news channel. Every now and then the younger, stronger, more classically handsome, de-aged Liam without all the scars and wounds of his life flashed on the screen.

It was almost impossible to believe he was the same tired, drained, exhausted, battered and bruised man sitting in front of her. It wasn't surprising that no one recognized him.

The gas-station map told them they were a little over three hours from Ottawa. The burgers arrived and Kelly watched as Liam created a pool of ketchup on the corner of his plate and dipped his burger in it as he ate. "You know, you're the only person I've ever known who does that."

Liam's eyebrows rose slightly. "Well, maybe other people do, but you haven't had burgers with them."

She smiled. "Yeah, probably."

He paused, then dipped his burger into the ketchup and took another bite.

"Did you ever get a cat?" he asked.

"I fostered some kittens for a while," she said. "I also had some birds. Do you still dislike cats?"

He laughed—it was a deep and warm chuckle that seemed to cut through space and time, back to when they'd sat in similar diners and had similar conversations all those years ago.

"Cats dislike me," he said. "Because they're sneaky and I see through them."

She laughed, too, and for a long moment neither of them said anything, they just ate from their shared basket of fries, their hands lightly bumping as they reached for them.

"I wanted to call when I heard your mom had passed away," Liam said. He looked down at the table. "I just didn't know what to say."

"She never really recovered from the shock of my dad laundering money and us being forced into witness protection," she said. "Didn't help my dad ran away with someone else. You said your dad passed?"

"Four years ago," Liam said. "It was cancer, pretty fast, but he had a few months in a hospice to tie up loose ends and say goodbyes."

Her hand reached for his across the

table and linked through his fingers. "I'm sorry."

"Thanks." Liam nodded. "Me, too."

"He must've been proud of all you've accomplished," she said.

"He was," Liam said. "This was all he ever wanted for me."

A silence fell between them again that was both comfortable and awkward at the same time, like a cross between a first date and catching up with an old friend. They left the diner ten minutes later, keeping their heads down and moving quickly. At first it seemed a choice between hitchhiking again or taking a bus. But then they spotted a beat-up car in front of someone's house with a for-sale sign on its windshield. The owner wanted fifteen hundred dollars for it, but Liam talked him down to nine hundred cash, and off they drove. They were down to their last few hundred dollars now, hardly enough for a few days' worth of food and a motel room each for them to sleep in when night fell. The car's summer tires were threadbare, the heater was broken and the right back-seat window was cracked. But it moved and it got them to Ottawa in time for the vigil.

And still her phone stayed silent. Had something happened to Renner? Had he been able to rescue Hannah? Worry permeated every beat of her heart, just like it had back in the day when she and Liam had first been on the run together. And yet, despite the pain, fear and uncertainty, she also knew there was no one else she'd rather have by her side.

A long, sprawling park ran along Ottawa's water's edge. Liam parked in a mostly empty lot and they walked, following a winding bike path. The faint sound of singing and gentle glow of lights rose ahead of them.

"Considering it's almost Christmas, there are probably several events going on in this park right now," Liam said. "I don't know how easy it's going to be to find this vigil, or even how many people are going to be there. I'm guessing no more than a dozen or so. Maybe less, considering the weather. But hopefully at least one member of my team will be there, or someone else I trust, and I'll be able to signal them." He frowned. "Although with Jess gone on her honeymoon, Noah getting married tomorrow and Mack hunkered down somewhere protecting Pip, there might not be."

They crested a hill as the sound of music seemed to swell and rise to meet them—the final verse of "Amazing Grace." Liam's footsteps faltered. Hundreds—no, thousands of candles were spread out in a rich tapestry of lights beneath them.

"This can't be it," Liam said. "This must be some kind of Christmas event and the vigil moved."

He turned as if to go. But Kelly's fingers grabbed hold of his and held fast.

"This is it," she said. "This is your candlelight vigil. All these people are here to celebrate you."

His head was shaking, but something in the slight quiver of his jaw as it set told her that he knew it was true.

"But they don't know me," he said. "They don't know anything about me. I'm a name on a police report or a tip sent their way."

"I know." Her hand tightened on his. He had no idea how honored she was that she got to know him and that out of all the lives he'd touched, she was the one person he'd opened up to, been vulnerable with and decided to love, no matter how fleeting their time together. "But you changed their lives and for some, they're only alive today because of you."

The music gave way to talking, as cop after cop spoke into a megaphone about Liam Bearsmith. And sure, it was clear most of them only knew of his uncanny knack for finding the right piece of evidence, pulling the right strings, finding the right source and showing up in the right place at the right time. They didn't know anything about his sense of humor, his insecurities or his heart. But the fact he'd existed, done his job and been dedicated to his work mattered to all of them.

And he was willing to give all this up for me.

Between the distance and the snow it was hard to get a good look at who was speaking as the megaphone was passed around. But there was something about the tone of the strong woman's voice when it took over the air that made Liam's back straighten.

"I'm detective Chloe Brant-Henry, OPP," she said.

"Wife of the man who left the message," Liam whispered.

"Liam and I worked a lot of cases together," Chloe said. "Some of them were incredible, hair-curling stuff, which you'll never get to hear about because they're above your pay grades." A ripple of laughter moved through the crowd. "When you grow up in a dysfunctional family, like my sister and I did, you learn to appreciate the family you find. As some of you know, when I married Trent I inherited three new brothers. What you probably don't know is that Liam has always been like an honorary brother to us. He's been there, without question, without hesitating, whenever we needed him. So wherever you are, Liam, I hope you know that you're our brother and we're here for you."

Liam pulled his fingers from hers and rubbed his hand across his eyes.

Her phone pinged, she pulled it out and glanced at the screen.

Hey, it's Renner. Got Hannah. She's safe. Locked onto your GPS in Ottawa now. On our way.
There in fifteen minutes. It's time to go.

"Renner has Hannah," Kelly said, glancing up at Liam from her phone. "She's safe and he's on his way to pick me up. He'll be here in fifteen minutes."

Renner was here? In Ottawa?

Liam felt himself blink. "What do you mean, he's on his way?"

"Apparently he can track my phone on GPS," Kelly said.

Since when? All this time he'd thought the phone was completely untraceable.

As he looked down at Kelly he could see the palpable relief and joy washing over her. He couldn't blame her. But something didn't sit right in Liam's core. Something felt off.

Help me, Lord. I've always been able to trust my gut. But right now I don't know what this thing is I'm feeling and it's clouding my vision.

"Come with me," Kelly said suddenly, as she pocketed her phone and then grabbed both of his hands in hers.

"What do you mean?" he asked.

"I mean…come with me." She said the words slowly. Her beautiful eyes locked on his face. "Come with Renner, Hannah, Pip and I. We'll all go hunker down together somewhere and sort out how to stop the Imposters and prove you're alive. You can get to know Renner and Hannah. We can figure this out together. Please, Liam, we've found each other again and I don't want to go without you."

Go with her? Leave his work? Just run away with Kelly and start a new life? She had no idea how much he'd been willing to throw everything away for her before. But now?

"I—I can't..." he said.

"You can." Something firm moved through her voice and for a moment he almost believed her. "Why not, Liam? Why not come with us?"

He wasn't even sure. He just knew whatever it was came from somewhere deep inside him he'd never tapped into before. "I have a life here. I have a team..."

"You *had* a life here," she said. "You had a team. But now your team is disbanding and everyone else thinks you're dead." She waved her hand toward the array of dazzling lights. "I'm not saying you shouldn't clear your name, prove you're alive and stop the Imposters. But why can't you do that with us? We can be your new team. We can go off-the-grid and find a way to do it together. For all your dedication to law enforcement, clearly somewhere along the line law enforcement let you down. Someone changed my file to keep us apart. Why not do what you wanted to do all those years ago—walk away from all this, and start again with me?"

I don't know! The words moved through him and he didn't know how to speak them. Kelly would never know how much he'd wanted a life with her then and was tempted to leave everything behind to start a new life with her now.

But he had no identification and no passport. His fingerprints matched a man who was wanted for murder. The only way to start anew with her was to go on the run and break the law.

"Because that's not the kind of man I

am," he said, the words crossing his lips the same moment they did his heart and mind. "Maybe it was never meant to be, as much as I wanted to give everything up to run away and be with you. This is my home, and this is my fight."

Her head was shaking and as he watched, a light dimmed in her eyes. Couldn't she see?

"You deserved a far better man than who I was when I asked you to marry me twenty-two years ago," he said. "You deserved a husband who didn't sneak around, break the rules and run from his responsibilities. You deserved a man who stepped up."

She pulled away, and as her eyes searched his face, they were filled with a look he couldn't quite decipher.

"And so, how are you going to be the kind of man who steps up now?" she asked.

That's just it. I don't know!

Before he could speak, her phone began

to ring. Kelly pulled it out and held it between them. "Hello?"

"Mom?" Hannah's voice floated into the night and suddenly Liam realized Kelly had put it on Speakerphone.

"Hannah?" Kelly's voice broke as her eyes flooded with tears. Immediately, Liam pressed his arm around the small of her back, supporting her weight as her limbs began to shake. "Is it really you?"

Silence fell on the other end of the line. A sob escaped Kelly's lips. Liam glanced around and spotted a snow-covered bench sitting in a pool of light under a lamppost. He led Kelly toward it, wiped it off and helped her sit. She clutched his arm.

"She's gone." Kelly looked up into his eyes. "It was Hannah. She was here and now she's gone."

"It's okay," Liam said. "She'll call back. The line must just be bad."

He glanced around and then he saw him. A lone figure standing by the road, not moving, not signaling him in any way, just staring at him. And even without seeing the man's face, he recognized his form in an instant.

It was Seth.

Liam stood. "I... Give me a second."

Her phone rang again.

"Hello?" Kelly answered it. "Hannah! Hi! Can you hear me? I can barely hear you."

She put it on Speakerphone so Liam could listen in.

"I'm here," Hannah said. "Stay where you are. We're driving your way."

Out of his peripheral vision, Liam could see Seth turn and walk toward the parking lot. He glanced from Kelly to Seth's disappearing form. *Help me, Lord! What do I do?*

"I'm here," Kelly told Hannah. "I can't wait to see you."

Seth was rapidly disappearing, but if Liam ran after him now he'd reach the other man in seconds.

"Stay here," Liam told Kelly. His hand

landed on her shoulder and his eyes locked on hers. "Right here. On this bench. Don't move. Don't go anywhere. And if anyone approaches you, scream. Okay?" She nodded. He glanced back—Seth had disappeared from sight. He turned back to Kelly. "I need you to promise me, if anyone approaches you, you'll scream for me and fight them off with all your might."

Kelly nodded. "I promise. Unless it's Hannah."

"Deal," he said, "unless it's Hannah. I'll be back in a second."

He brushed a kiss over the top of her head and bolted after Seth. For a moment he thought he'd lost him altogether. Then he spotted the hacker walking between the vehicles in a half-empty parking lot.

"Seth!" Liam shouted. "Stop!"

The hacker turned, his hood fell back and Seth's eyes widened. Then Seth began to run. *No!* Whatever was going on, Seth was not getting away now. Liam pressed his body forward, his feet pounding on the icy ground as he ran after his former teammate. Within moments Liam had caught him—he grabbed Seth's coat at the back of his neck and spun him around.

"I'm sorry," Seth said, his eyes wide. "I really am. I can explain."

"Not good enough," Liam growled. He let Seth go and watched as the hacker's knees buckled. "I thought we were on the same team."

"We are!" Guilt flooded Seth's face. "It's just, a buddy asked me for help and I had to help him."

"Who?" Liam demanded. "Who are you helping?"

Too late, he felt the prick of a mini–stun gun against the back of his neck. Seth was bait. The real threat was standing behind him.

"He's helping me." A voice—male, young and unfamiliar—filled his ear as electricity shot through Liam, bringing him to his knees.

ELEVEN

"Hello?" Kelly called into the phone. "Hello?"

She glanced around the empty winter night. The music from the vigil had surged. Hannah's voice had been there a moment ago and now she was gone again. And Kelly couldn't see Liam anywhere.

"I'm almost there." Hannah's voice was back in her ear. "Can you walk down the road and we'll meet you there?"

"I…" She swallowed hard. If she left now she might never see Liam again. That was more than she was willing to risk. "I'm sorry, I can't. I need to wait for Liam. He—he did a really great job of taking care of Pip."

No answer. Just more crackling came

down the line. She sighed. Kelly wasn't sure what to make of the fact Hannah hadn't asked about her daughter yet. But it was possible she was worried the call was being hacked somehow. Not to mention the signal kept cutting out and they'd barely exchanged a handful of sentences. Her phone had almost no bars. If only she hadn't promised Liam she'd stay on the bench, she'd go wander for a better signal. She glanced to the streetlamp behind her. Then again, she hadn't agreed to anything about how she'd stay on the bench. She stood up, bracing her feet on the slippery metal seat, and leaned against the lamppost. Bingo. She now had another bar. Not to mention a better view. She could now see the road on one side, cold and white, and the glittering candlelight vigil on the other. But she still couldn't see Liam anywhere.

"Okay, we'll come find you," Hannah said. "Just driving down the road toward your GPS signal now."

Okay, but where was Liam? Even if he didn't come with her, even if this was the last time they saw each other again, she wasn't about to let him leave her life without saying goodbye. And asking him to please find a way for them to stay in each other's lives. She closed her eyes and prayed.

I lost him once, Lord. I can't lose him again.

"I need a minute," Kelly said. "Liam just needed to sort something, and I promised I wouldn't go anywhere without telling him."

"We don't have a minute," Hannah said.

A horn honked and Kelly turned to see a black SUV with tinted windows pulling up on the road. Faint snow blew between her and the van, catching the light like glitter. The driver was a dark and featureless shape. Then the van's back door slid open, and she saw the young woman sitting in the back seat, her figure silhouetted in the van's interior seat. And even though she couldn't see clearly from the distance, snow and combination of darkness and shadows, Kelly's heart leaped.

It was her daughter. It was Hannah. Safe, alive and in one piece.

She leaped off the bench and jogged toward her, across the snowy ground.

"We've got to go." Hannah's voice came through the cell phone and Kelly wondered if she was intentionally keeping her voice low instead of yelling out.

Come on, Liam. Where are you?

"I don't want to leave without Liam," she admitted.

"Where is he?" Hannah's voice came through the phone.

"I don't know," Kelly said. "Somewhere close. It's a long story."

"Just get in the van and we'll drive around and look for him."

Her eyes glanced to the falling snow and to the sky above.

Help me, Lord. If I leave now, will I ever find him again?

"Let's go!" Hannah called.

Kelly's footsteps faltered. Something was wrong. Her daughter's tone was off and now that she was closer she could tell her daughter's body had barely flinched. She stopped. "What's wrong?"

"Nothing's wrong," her daughter's calm voice said on the phone.

Yet, as she watched, Hannah's body moved, and she was tossing her head violently and jerking toward Kelly as if forcing her unwilling limbs to move. And then Kelly saw it.

Hannah's mouth was gagged.

The voice on the phone had been a deep fake, just like the video of Liam. Hannah wasn't safe. She wasn't with Renner. The Imposters still had her. Hannah's desperate eyes met Kelly's, as if silently begging her to run.

I will. I'll find your father. And then I'll find you again.

Kelly turned and ran, her feet crunching over the snow. Behind her she could hear van doors opening and people pounding after her.

"Liam!" she screamed, feeling his name rip from her throat. "Help me!"

She had to find him. She had to reach him before it was too late.

A sudden body blow came from behind as one of the Imposters tackled her. It was too late. She fell forward, her body hitting hard against the snowy ground. She thrashed hard, trying desperately to fight. But there were too many of them. One Imposter was pushing her down. A second was tying a gag around her mouth, silencing her screams and barely giving her time to clench her jaw the way Liam had told her about. A third tied her hands behind her back. Then she felt her body yanked backward, half-carried and half-dragged through the snow. Her body was flung into a seat beside Hannah. The SUV doors closed. Kelly met her daughter's eyes. Their shoulders leaned into each other, as mother and daughter silently passed each other faith, strength and hope.

The van drove off into the night.

Please, Lord, may someone find us before it's too late.

Of all the problems Liam had envisioned when Seth had joined their team, finding himself stunned and dragged into the back of a freezing van by some unseen accomplice hadn't exactly been at the top of the list. But now, as Liam's head was beginning to clear and he could feel the cold metal beneath his knees and hear the wind whistling through a cracked door, he suddenly realized that he cared a whole lot less about the identity of the unknown man behind him, who had one gloved hand clamped on Liam's shoulder and the other holding a knife to his throat, than he did about the hacker now crouched on the van floor in front of him. The man behind him, whoever he was, was just one more threat and menace in a long line of people who'd tried to take Liam's life over the years.

But Seth was something far more important.

"Believe it or not, Seth," Liam said, "I cared about you and I respected you. I considered you a friend. So whatever this is, it's low. Even for you."

Seth rocked back on his heels and his face paled so suddenly it was like Liam's words had actually winded him. "You've never called me a friend before."

"And you've never kidnapped me!" Liam's voice rose. "Now are you going to tell your buddy here to let me go and explain why you joined forces with the Imposters and what it is you think you're doing? Or do I have to break his arm, risk getting myself stabbed and fight my way out of here?"

Seth cast a glance at whoever was still holding Liam hostage at knifepoint. The figure was a man, judging by both the grip and the voice he'd previously heard. There appeared to just be the three of them.

"Let him go," Seth told the man.

"Not yet," the man behind Liam said. "Not until we've talked things out and know for sure whose side he's on."

"You want to know what side I'm on?" Liam snapped. "I'm on the side of both following the law and taking care of the people I care about."

He had to get back to Kelly. It had only been a few minutes since he'd left her alone on the bench. But a lot could happen in a few minutes. He gritted his teeth. Then again, it always amazed him how much intel he could get out of someone who was threatening his life. He prayed for wisdom and listened to his instincts. Maybe he didn't need to be told what was going on.

Maybe there was only one answer that explained everything. But was he right?

"Fine, I'll listen," Liam said. "But not while Kelly's in danger. Because I left her, out there on a bench, talking to Hannah on the phone and waiting for Renner to pick her up."

There was a sharp intake of breath from the man behind him and the knife flinched half an inch away from his throat. But it wasn't enough. Not yet.

"Actually, I owe you an apology, Seth," Liam said. "I haven't been fully honest with you. I'm not the clean-nosed, by-the-book guy everyone thinks I am. I made a major mistake years ago, one that by rights should've derailed my career if someone hadn't altered Kelly's witness-protection files to cover it up. Kelly and I were romantically involved. I asked her to marry me. I thought she moved on without me. What I didn't know is we had a daughter. Her name was Hannah Phillips. I'm Hannah's biological father. Her daughter, Pip, is my granddaughter, and Kelly is the only woman I ever fell for. And no matter what ridiculous story you're about to tell me, I'm not about to let anything happen to them."

This time the knife fell ever farther from his neck. The hand gripping his shoulder began to shake. There, now that was the signal he was waiting for.

Liam struck, grabbed the knife with both hands and spun hard to the side. He slammed the offending arm against the side of the van wall, forcing the knife to fall from the man's grasp. Then he glanced at his kidnapper. The man was of average height, average build and masked. Also seemed he wasn't about to give up that easily. The man swung. Liam rolled out of the way and almost made it, absorbing the glancing blow in his shoulder.

Liam almost sighed. He was getting too old for this.

"Stop!" Liam shouted, crouching up on his feet and holding up his hands. "I get that you're scared, desperate or whatever it is that's motivating you right now. But you really think three grown men throwing punches in the back of a van is going to solve anything?"

"Hey, *I* wasn't about to punch anyone," Seth muttered.

Maybe not, but the masked man was about to try to. Liam ducked his blow, shoved him back against the van wall and yanked off the man's mask.

"Renner Phillips, right?" Liam said. Renner nodded without answering. "Rumor has it you're dead. But that seems to be catching right now."

"Where's my daughter?" Renner demanded.

"Safe." Liam sat back without letting Renner up fully. The curly-haired young man looked younger than Liam expected and every bit as desperate as Liam had felt when he'd first realized, so long ago, that he was falling in love with a woman whose life was in danger.

"I get why you're an emotional, irrational wreck," Liam added. "If what you feel for my daughter is half what I felt for her mama then your brain is a mess right now. And that's not even considering Pip. The woman and baby you love are in danger. I feel that. So, I understand why you're being dumb." Liam let out a long breath. Then he glanced at Seth. "You, on the other hand, should've known better."

Seth opened his mouth, like some big explanation was hovering on his tongue, then wisely thought twice and shut it again.

"Now, if I didn't need your help, I'd arrest you both," Liam said. "Even without a badge and presumed dead." He looked at Renner. "Please tell me that you've been texting Kelly, you rescued Hannah and she's filling Kelly in on everything right now."

Renner shook his head. "I haven't been texting Kelly. Her phone was compromised and I had to go dark. I don't know where Hannah is. The Imposters have her."

That was what Liam had been afraid of.

"I tried to tell you not to use that phone," Seth said.

Liam leaped out of the van.

"I'm getting Kelly," Liam called, turning his back on the men his brain wanted to interrogate and instead following his heart. "I left her on that bench talking to who-knows-who. Join me if you want or run off and keep up with whatever foolish thing you think you're doing. I don't have time to try and stop you. Not while she's out there alone."

He sprinted across the snowy ground, back toward where he'd left Kelly.

Lord, please help me get there in time. Please keep Kelly safe.

He pushed through the snow, hearing the other two men running behind him. A motor sounded in the distance. He reached the bench and sank to his knees.

Kelly was gone, leaving nothing but the signs of a struggle spreading out like ugly gashes in the snow where Kelly had fought for her life.

He looked up as Renner and Seth reached his side.

"You're going to tell me how to find her."

TWELVE

A few minutes later, the three men sat in a diner. It was the kind with stained mugs, cracked saltshakers and faded vinyl tablecloths that looked like they hadn't been changed in so long they were now melded to the table. It also was the type of place where nobody looked at another person twice and the waitstaff ignored you unless called. Liam had met with dozens of informants in this exact place and countless others like it, while wearing all number of different personas. But not once had he done so with his heart burning like a furnace inside him, threatening to consume his rational mind.

He glanced from Renner to Seth and back.

"So," Liam said. "The Imposters still

have Hannah and presumably now have Kelly, too. Her supposedly secure phone was compromised this whole time and Renner was never messaging Kelly."

He thanked God the phone's battery was dead for as long as it was.

"The world thinks you're dead and took your special master-key decryption device to the grave," he continued. "The Imposters don't believe that, though, and are willing to cause chaos to get their hands on it." He reminded himself Kelly said there was no decipher key. "And the world still thinks I'm dead," he added. "Now you two are going to help me fill in the gaps."

"Are you sure my daughter is safe?" Renner asked.

It wasn't the first time he'd asked the question, but it was about time Liam did more than give him an answer.

"Yes," Liam said. But before he put Renner's heart at ease, he had to ask Seth something. He turned to the hacker.

"Please tell me you're not a criminal, you had a really good reason for letting the Imposters kidnap Kelly and I and that you're about to convince me to trust you."

Seth nodded. "Yes. I promise."

Liam believed him. "Then text Mack and tell him where we are and who's with us."

He turned back to Renner. "Now, fill me in."

"What makes you think you're Hannah's father?" Renner asked. His voice was so stretched thin with stress Liam was surprised it hadn't snapped.

Fair question, Liam thought. It's not every day a man accidentally kidnapped and tried to fight his father-in-law.

"Kelly said I was," Liam said, "and that's all the proof I needed."

She was the first person he'd ever trusted implicitly. He glanced from Seth to the twenty-four-hour television screen now showing his own vigil. Kelly had been the first. But maybe not the only one.

"Seth," Liam said. The hacker glanced up from his phone. "Like I told you, I had an inappropriate and secret relationship with Kelly when I was a rookie. If word had gotten out, I'd have faced even more severe consequences than Mack did and my career would've taken a major hit. I might've even been fired. Instead, someone blocked her attempts to contact me and her RCMP file was changed. I trust you can figure out how and why."

Although he suspected he didn't want to know the answer.

Liam turned back to Renner. "I care about Kelly. I've risked my life to protect her, Hannah and Pip, and I will do everything in my power to ensure they're safe. Now talk." As much as he was dying to ask Renner how he'd broken the code, his gut told him Renner wasn't about to tell him that yet. "You hacked an unbreakable code. Then what happened?"

"My life changed instantly," Renner said. His face paled at the memory. "My email, phone and social media were flooded with job offers and people trying to buy my method, which was overwhelming. Some were really pushy. But what was far worse were the threats. All these anonymous accounts and criminal groups were threatening to find my wife and do terrible things to her if I didn't give them the master key."

"And you didn't trust the government to keep you safe?"

"My vehicle blew up!" Renner barely caught himself from raising his voice. "If someone could do that to me, who's to say they couldn't do worse to Hannah. She was only a few weeks pregnant with Pip."

So Hannah had gone into RCMP witness protection and Renner had gone underground.

"Then when the original Imposters stole the RCMP witness-protection database a few weeks later, you knew people would be looking for Hannah's identity," Liam said, "so you got Kelly to get to her file first. Someone had to talk her through how to do it. She couldn't have done it herself. Was it you?"

Renner shook his head. Liam glanced at Seth.

The hacker raised his hands. "It wasn't me."

Okay, that he believed, too. So who was left then?

"So," Liam continued, "then the original two Imposters died in a shoot-out with our friends Noah and Holly. Everything dies down. You decide instead of coming forward, you're going to try to set up a new life somewhere, off-the-grid, with Hannah and Pip, where you'll all be safe. Then a bunch of copycat Imposters emerged, and they decided they wanted your nonexistent decipher key. Got all that right?"

Renner sat there stone-faced. Liam took that as a yes.

He rested his elbows on the table and leaned in toward Seth.

"Now, where did you two meet?" he asked.

"Online," Seth said. "I've been curious about Renner for a while, found him online, told him about my own background and offered to give him a hand if he needed it. We have similar backgrounds and I figured we were like-minded individuals."

Liam ran his hand over his face and wished he was more surprised by this. "So, you've been talking to a wanted man online?"

"Our team wasn't investigating him," Seth said. His chin rose. "And considering my own past, I really related to his decision to drop off-the-grid. I thought maybe I could talk him into trusting us. Besides, I didn't know where in the world he was and we never met in person or had a real conversation until Hannah was kidnapped and he asked me for my help."

Renner nodded, confirming Seth's account. Liam didn't like it. But he believed it.

Then again, if Liam himself hadn't been so stubbornly independent, would Seth have trusted him with this earlier?

"Okay, and why do people think you're an Imposter?" Liam asked.

To his surprise, Seth blushed slightly. "Because I am. Sort of."

"You're what?" Liam felt his voice rise to a roar. Of all the possible answers, he hadn't been expecting that one. Other patrons swiveled their eyes their way for an instant, and then back to their own business. Liam forced his voice to drop. "Care to explain?"

"I went undercover," Seth said. "Without authorization. But I'm a hacker, right? Not a cop. I told you these new Imposters are decentralized. They have no leader. Nobody is in charge. I was monitoring their group, saw the opportunity and I took it. But that still doesn't mean I know what's going on more than any other person on that site. I found out about the attack on the boat about two minutes before it went down. It's all splinter cells."

Liam ran his hand over the back of his neck. "Does this mean you can shut them down?"

"Hypothetically," Seth said. "But it would take some serious computer power, a way to get into the code behind their main system and at least three of me."

So that would be a no.

"Why did you sell Kelly and I out at the church?" Liam asked.

"Because somebody tracked you to Tatlow's Used Books when Kelly's phone came online," Seth said. "I was in the area. I wanted to catch a glimpse of the family from afar, even if I couldn't be there. I saw you leave a baby in the apartment with Mack and Iris. Then I saw the Imposters show up. They were going to storm the building and put the kid in danger. More importantly, there was no indication the Imposters even knew about the baby. It seemed like the smartest way to rescue her. I figured there wouldn't be that many of them, I could lure them to the church, get there first and then you'd do your thing and take them down. When we were outnumbered, I improvised, did what I had to do to maintain my cover and then took the car you were in out remotely. Which, unfortunately, took a lot longer than I expected."

"Which is why people shouldn't go off-the-grid and try to take the law into their own hands," Liam said. He felt his eyes narrow. "They paid you off."

"You think I cared about the money?" Seth said. "I wanted the electronic transfer to back-channel into the cell phone of whoever took the money. I've managed to pinpoint it down to a general geographic area near Lake Simcoe, which tells us practically nothing."

"Which tells us a lot," Liam said. "Because Noah and Holly, who fired the shots that took down the original Imposters, are getting married in that area tomorrow.

Might give these new Imposters a nice opportunity to achieve both their goals of getting Renner to hand over the non-existent decryption key and get revenge on my team on Christmas Eve."

So Seth had slid backward and foolishly tried to solve crime his old, independent and vigilante way. And Renner was so focused on protecting the woman and child he loved he went off-the-grid and let his emotion overwhelm his judgment.

But there was still one piece of the picture he didn't have.

Liam leaned his elbows on the table and fixed his eyes on Renner.

"I believe you love my daughter and my granddaughter," Liam said. "I believe you'd do anything to protect them. So I'll ask you, one more time, man to man—if there was never a master-key decoding device, how did you break that code?"

Something hardened in Renner's face, like an invisible steel trap dropping over his eyes, locking Liam out.

Something jangled behind him. Liam turned and glanced down the back hallway. There stood Iris, half-hidden in the shadows and yet with an unmistakable smile on her face.

"Come on," Liam said softly, gesturing for Renner to follow him. "There's someone you need to meet."

The three of them stood and walked through the diner and out into the back hallway. There by the open back door stood Mack, with baby Pip in his arms.

Her little eyes opened wide. Her arms stretched out toward them as a happy squeal slipped from her lips. He heard a sob escape from the back of Renner's throat and for the first time since they'd met, Liam watched all bravado fall from Renner's eyes.

"Is that..." Two words were all Renner got out before emotion swallowed up the rest.

"Your daughter?" Liam said softly, feeling something well up in his own voice. "Yeah, that's your little girl."

He watched as Renner ran down the hallway, swept the baby up into his arms and cradled her to his chest. Prayers of thanks poured from the man's lips as he held his baby girl for the very first time.

Liam turned away, feeling tears brush the corners of his own eyes.

He looked at Seth, Mack and Iris.

"Renner's telling the truth when he says he doesn't have a master-key decryption device," Liam said. "I wasn't sure what I believed about that. But that man would give absolutely anything for his wife and baby."

"What does that mean?" Seth asked.

"We have to get creative if we want to get Hannah and Kelly back alive." Liam stretched out his hand for Seth's cell phone, and when the hacker gave it to him, Liam opened a new message and typed.

It's me, Liam. I'm alive. I need your help. I need a team.

He needed a family.

* * *

Kelly was lying on the cold concrete floor in the darkness, surrounded by the smell of hay and earth, feeling the warmth of Hannah leaning against her back. She had no idea how many hours it had been since she'd been kidnapped in the park. They'd been in the car for at least four, she guessed, before the vehicle had pulled up outside what appeared to be large abandoned stables in the middle of nowhere, surrounded by nothing but snow and trees.

Then they'd been shoved into a narrow stall where they were lying on the floor, napping in fits and starts, slowly working their gags away from their mouths and pulling at the bonds holding each other's hands whenever whatever Imposter was on sentry duty walked out of view. Although clenching her jaw had helped Kelly some, it'd still taken her a long time to work it free enough to speak, especially as they were being watched.

Mostly she'd prayed. She prayed for her

and Hannah's safety, and for Renner and Pip. She prayed that every single Imposter would be stopped and caught, no matter where they were in the world.

And she prayed for Liam, asking God to clear his name, guard his life and give him an amazing future.

"I'm sorry, Mom," Hannah's muffled voice behind her let her know her daughter was awake. "This is all my fault."

"Stop saying that," Kelly whispered firmly. Hannah had been trying to apologize ever since she'd been able to speak. But between the gag still in her mouth and the tiny windows of time they had to talk, Kelly still didn't know why. "None of this is your fault."

Footsteps drew nearer as their latest guard grew closer. Kelly was still. Her fingers squeezed Hannah's. The guard passed. The women went back to trying to loosen each other's bonds. She'd searched the floor the best she could for anything sharp she could loop the bonds around to rip them free but hadn't found anything yet. When Liam had told her how to break free from gags and bonds, he hadn't explained just how long it could take.

"Listen, I'm sorry I never told you that Liam was your father," Kelly said. "He's a good man. He took care of Pip and me. He would've loved you."

"Did he love you?" Hannah asked.

Kelly swallowed hard and sudden tears rushed to her eyes, as she finally let her heart acknowledge the truth she hadn't for far too long. "He did. The very best he could."

And I loved him. Liam had been the love of her life.

Voices rose from elsewhere in the stables. Footsteps stomped down the floor toward them. Something crashed. She looked up. Three masked Imposters stood in front of them. Two held guns. The third grabbed them each by an arm and yanked them up.

"Come on." The voice was male and young. "Time for a show."

They were marched down the hall into a large room with a huge double door. In the middle of the room sat a folding table with a couple of chairs and multiple laptops. She counted about a dozen masked and armed men standing around it, but it wasn't until the crowd parted that she saw the one unmasked man standing in their midst.

It was Seth.

"Hey." Seth waved nervously in their direction. There was a small bright red and cylindrical memory drive in his hand. "So, funny story. I managed to track Renner down and get my hands on Renner's supersecret master-key decryption device. Figured out where these guys were holding you, based on some pretty savvy old-school detective work, came here and offered to trade your lives for the decipher key. Turns out this disorganized gang isn't big on making deals or loyalty. Mob rule, eh?"

Old-school detective work. The words jolted Kelly's heart, sending hope beating through it. Did that mean Liam had helped him? Was Liam there?

One man ordered Seth into a chair. Another held a gun to the back of his head. Voices rose as Imposters argued amongst themselves. It sounded as if they'd agreed on forcing Seth to hack into the Bank of Canada to prove his decipher key was legit and would shoot Kelly, Hannah and Seth himself if he couldn't. Specifically, they wanted him to go after the $888 million that the bank had collected from closed and unclaimed bank accounts across the country and was now holding in reserve as it awaited the rightful heirs and owners of that money to come claim it. Although, the Imposters couldn't quite agree on how much of those millions he should steal or how many accounts that money should be transferred into. Seth looked down at the laptop and sighed. A weary look crossed his face.

"Believe it or not," he said, "this is not the first or even fourth time I've been stuck in a chair, in front of a laptop, at gunpoint. Twice, I've even had a bomb strapped to me." The hacker's eyes closed. "God, this has gotta be the last time I go through this," he prayed out loud. "I'm sorry for all the stupid choices that led me here. So if You're there, and I get out of this alive, please help me make whatever changes I need to to make sure this never happens to me again."

The honesty and simplicity of his prayer made something catch in her throat.

"You have fifteen minutes to break in," an Imposter said, jabbing his finger at the screen. "After that, I start shooting hostages."

Kelly's eyes scanned the barn, looking at one Imposter after another, hoping against hope to spot Liam's strong form under one of the masks. She couldn't see him anywhere. And yet somehow she knew, with every beat of her heart, that Liam was close, and one way or another he would find her.

Help us, Lord! Please get us out of this alive!

Then she saw the rough metal hook behind her on the wall, bent and rusty with age. She backed up toward it. Seth stuck the memory drive into one of the laptops and started typing. His hands shook and his face was pale, and suddenly she realized Seth didn't actually have the decoding device. The hacker had been faking it and now he was going to die for it. Kelly's bound hands snagged on the hook. Desperate prayers poured through her.

"No! It was me!" The muffled words ripped through Hannah's gag in a panicked cry. "It was me! It was me!"

What was she doing? Instinctively Kelly started toward her daughter, but her snagged hands held her back. A masked

Imposter grabbed Hannah with one hand and yanked the gag from her mouth.

"It was me!" Hannah shouted. "It was me. There was no master-key decryption device. There never was. I hacked the code."

Hannah gasped a panicked breath. The Imposters's voices moved in a babble of confusion around her.

"Stop this now," Hannah said. "Please. Let him go. There was no decipher key. It was only me." Hannah spun back and her eyes met Kelly's. "I've been hacking codes for Renner for a long time, even though I didn't have security clearance. I didn't want to have to work a high-pressure government-contractor job like that. I saw what it did to Renner. So I thought he could sneak me codes every now and then and I'd decode them, and no one would have to know. But then it got too big and things went wrong. I'm so sorry, Mom. Renner was trying to protect me."

Hannah's chin rose. Pride mingled with

the fear in her gaze. And Kelly saw what her heart had been hiding from her all this time. Liam's voice floated in the back of her mind.

Foolish kids in love don't always make the best decisions.

"Stop!" Kelly called through her gag. "Please!"

But it was too late. The masked men were already forcing Hannah into another chair and turning another laptop toward her. Arguments rose among the masked men about their new plan. Some decided they'd shoot whichever one didn't break into the Bank of Canada first. Others thought they should both be shot if they didn't start the online heist within fifteen minutes.

The metal hook pressed against Kelly's fingers. Absolutely no one was looking at her and again Liam's voice hovered in the back of her mind, reminding her to never miss an opportunity to use distraction.

She gritted her teeth and prayed that she

was physically and emotionally strong enough to do what she was about to do. Then she lunged forward, pain shooting through her arms as she felt the already weakened bonds rip away from her wrists. Her hands fell free. She turned and ran, bolting back down the hallway.

A doorway loomed ahead, showing a glimmer of pale gray morning light. Shouting sounded behind her. She didn't let herself look back. Instead, she burst through the barn door and out into the snow, and ran up the hill in front of her.

Fields of white filled her vision on all sides. There was no Liam, no rescue, no buildings, nothing but endless snow with a fringe of trees on the horizon. She was all alone. Liam wasn't there. He hadn't come to save her.

Then she saw the truck, white and dingy with snow, sitting at the crest of the hill, half-hidden in the trees. She ran for it.

THIRTEEN

"I think maybe we've got a runner," Renner said. He leaned on the steering wheel with one hand and peered through the binoculars. Seth had pointed out that the same kind of electronic tracking methods he'd used to locate the stables could be used against them in reverse. So they hadn't so much as used a cell phone since reaching the location, let alone any high-tech tracking devices. It had been ten long hours since Kelly had been kidnapped and Liam still wasn't sure what he thought of his newfound son-in-law. Renner was reckless, selfish and stubborn. When Liam had finally gotten Renner to confess that Hannah had broken the code, that he'd been secretly passing her codes for months and he'd let rumors of some magical decoding device proliferate to keep from putting a target on her back, Liam suddenly felt the desire to knock Renner and Hannah's heads together for being so reckless, along with the competing urge to hug them and tell them that he understood. Maybe that was what being a father was like. Also, Liam kind of liked him.

"Maybe?" Liam asked.

"Definitely," Renner said. "Headed straight at us."

"Let me see." Liam stuck out his hand, Renner passed him the binoculars and in a single glance, Liam knew what he was looking at. "It's Kelly!"

He tossed the binoculars at Renner and leaped out. "Cover me!"

"Cover you?" Renner shouted. "You're out in the open running through an open field! If someone comes after you, you're a sitting duck!"

Yeah, but so was Kelly. And he was going to be her cover and protection.

Liam raced down the hill, running toward Kelly with all his might. Yes, he knew that running right into danger was breaking one of his father's most important rules of staying alive. But for the first time since he'd first kissed Kelly's lips and asked her to marry him, over twenty years ago, Liam knew he was heading in the right direction with nothing holding him back. He raced through the snow, pushing his body toward her, as he watched her run for him.

"Liam!" Her voice called for him, the sound muffled—he could see she was gagged.

"Kelly!" He felt her name explode through his core, like it was coming from somewhere deeper than the breath in his lungs. "I'm coming!"

They pressed closer. His heart ached with each step. Then he reached her and swept her up into his arms. He ripped the gag free from her mouth and kissed her, feeling her arms lock around his neck.

"I love you." The words flew from Liam's lips the moment their kiss ended. "I'm in love with you, Kelly, and I have been forever."

"I know," Kelly said. "Because I love you, too."

"Incoming!" Renner shouted.

Liam swung Kelly behind him, positioning himself between her and the approaching Imposter. Liam fired, catching the man in the arm and robbing his ability to aim and fire back. The Imposter fell into the snow.

Then Liam wrapped one arm around her shoulders and ran with her back to the truck.

"Hannah's in the barn," she shouted to Renner as Liam yanked open the door and they tumbled into the passenger seat, and he pulled Kelly onto his lap. "She and Seth are both hacking." She glanced at Liam. "Did you know?"

"That she's the hacker and there was

no decipher key?" Liam asked. "Yeah, Renner told me, eventually."

"Well, Hannah told the Imposters," she said.

Renner took in a sharp breath. Kelly spun her head toward him.

"If I was the kind of person who hit people I'd have a hard time not smacking you right now!" she said. "You violated security clearance and broke the law by letting Hannah even see high-security codes, let alone crack one for you. You put Hannah and Pip in danger. You kept the truth from me!"

Her words tapered off as Renner's face went pale.

"I love your daughter," he said. "I did what I thought I needed to do to protect her."

She let out a long breath.

"I know," she said. "And I forgive you. Now, we've got to focus on saving her."

She brushed her lips across Liam's cheek

in a fleeting kiss and then she climbed in the back seat.

"We've got to get in there," she said. "They told Hannah and Seth if they don't break into the Bank of Canada and rob it in fifteen minutes they're going to start shooting people, and we're down to like six minutes now. What's the old-school way of stopping killer hackers in a barn?"

Liam and Renner exchanged a glance. Then Liam nodded and Renner revved his engine.

"Buckle your seat belt," Liam said.

Kelly did so. Then she felt Liam reach back and squeeze her hand.

"How far away are Hannah and Seth from the barn door?" Renner asked.

"Maybe thirty feet?" she said. "They're seated at a table."

"Anyone want to get out before we do this?" Liam asked. "Not going to pretend crashing a truck through a barn door isn't dangerous."

"I definitely won't be any safer running down the hill without cover than staying in here," Kelly said, "especially if they open fire on us. Hannah's in there, and I'm the only one who knows what the layout is. I'm not staying behind."

"Neither am I," Renner said. "Hannah's your daughter, but she's also my wife."

"Stay low," Liam said, "and brace for impact."

Renner hit the gas. Liam's hand tightened on hers for a fleeting moment, then let go, and she braced herself against the back of his seat. The truck flew down the hill, plowing through the snow and picking up speed as it went. Her prayers mingled with Liam's as the barn grew closer.

Forty feet. Thirty feet. Twenty feet. Ten.

Then Renner hit the brakes and the truck spun sideways in a controlled skid as it crashed through the barn doors. Instinctively, she unbuckled her seat belt and ducked low beneath the seat as the sounds

of shouting, crashing, banging and gunfire surrounded her.

"Try to rescue Hannah and Seth if you
can," Liam shouted. "Renner and I will
take out the Imposters."

Doors slammed, she looked up and
found herself alone in the truck. She
scrambled into the driver's seat and
watched the scene unfolding around her in
the stables, like something out of a dance
choreography, as both Liam and Renner
moved in tandem to take cover, surge forward, fire and then fall back, taking out
one Imposter after another with a skill and
precision that took her breath away. Liam
was clearly leading, with Renner following close behind, as if the men had known
each other for years instead of hours.

*Thank You, God, that Liam didn't give
up law enforcement for me. This is who
he is. This is where he belongs.*

Kelly scanned the room and spotted
Hannah and Seth, crouched side by side,
underneath the table. They were both still

typing madly. The truck's keys hung from the ignition. Kelly started the engine and inched through the chaos toward them, placing the truck between the hackers and the battle, even as she heard the sound of bullets pinging off the other side of the truck. She shoved open the back door.

"Get in!" she shouted.

They crawled toward her, staying low and dragging their laptops with them.

"Everybody good?" Kelly called.

"Yeah," Hannah said.

The clacking of keys grew louder. She glanced back. Seth and Hannah were both still typing, sitting on the floor behind the seats.

"What are you doing?" Kelly called.

"We've hacked inside the Imposters's online system," Hannah said, without looking up.

"I knew if they made us hack they'd accidentally let us in," Seth said. His eyes were equally locked on the screen. "This is the opportunity we've been waiting for."

"You're able to stop their threat to take down power grids on New Year's Eve?" Kelly asked.

A smile curved on Hannah's lips.

"We're able to take down everything," Hannah said. "Every single thing is going down and for good."

"Everything?" Kelly asked.

"We're in their membership database right now," Seth said. "Back-channeling Imposters from their online signatures to find their real names, locations and addresses. Basically, everything the police will need to find each and every one of them, and take down their organization."

Hannah laughed under her breath. Despite the chaos around them, the light in Hannah's eyes was pure determination and joy. After all their months apart, had Hannah and Renner even seen each other in the chaos, let alone managed to say anything? She didn't know. But here her daughter was, taking out criminals online while her husband was outside doing the same in his own way. This was who her daughter was. This was the woman she and Liam had made, and who'd been raised by the incredible and loving couple who'd adopted her. This was who she was meant to be.

"When we get out of here, I want you and Renner to come forward," Kelly said. Hannah looked up and met her eyes. "I know it'll be hard and scary, there might be ramifications and it'll change your lives. But look at you. You're amazing. You're happy. You're incredible. You love this, don't you? I don't want you to hide from who you are."

Hannah nodded slightly, then she looked back to the screen.

Too late, Kelly heard the truck door wrenched open to her left. She looked up to see one of the Imposters, hulking, huge and masked, looming over her. She screamed, yelling to Hannah and Seth to stay down and safe, as she felt the masked Imposter cuffing her hard against her temple and yanking her from the truck. She fell and her body smacked hard against the cold stable floor, knocking the breath from her lungs. Then she felt the Imposter dragging her across the floor, toward the stable's stalls. Kelly kicked and screamed, thrashing and fighting against her attacker with every ounce of strength in her body. Her eyes searched in vain for Liam in the chaos. She couldn't see him anywhere. Desperate tears filled her eyes.

Then she heard Liam's voice, like a deep and guttural roar. "Get your hands off her!"

And it was like her attacker was literally lifted off the ground, as Liam yanked the man off her and tossed him to the side. The Imposter scrambled away and disappeared back into the chaos.

She looked up and there Liam stood, protecting her and shielding her, placing himself between her and those who wanted to hurt her.

"Are you okay?" Liam asked. She nodded, as he pulled her up into his chest, placing one strong hand at the small of her back and keeping his weapon at the ready with the other. He led her backward into one of the stalls.

"How did you find me?" she asked. "How did you even know I was in danger?"

He looked down at her and something deepened in his gaze.

"Sweetheart, I'm always going to be looking out for you."

A shiver ran through her body that seemed to seep deep into her core.

She glanced past him. Renner was pinned down in a corner fighting off several Imposters at once. Others were now advancing on the truck, where Seth and Hannah were still hunkered down in the back.

"We have to help them!" she said. "They're sitting ducks!"

But even as she spoke, she heard a chorus of shouts and watched as Liam's team members Jess and Noah, along with almost a dozen other men and women, stormed through the entrances like a precision team and quickly moved to secure the scene. For a moment they just watched as the team moved in, covering Renner's back, protecting the truck and arresting Imposters. Then she felt a long sigh move through Liam. He holstered his weapon.

"I texted a few friends last night," Liam said. He wrapped both arms around her, and nestled her into his chest. "They've got this."

"Who are they?" Wonder filled her voice. "What is this?"

"The three other detectives helping Jess and Noah round up and cuff suspects are Chloe and Trent Henry and Trent's brother, Jacob," he said "Chloe's provincial and the other two are federal."

"I thought Jess left for her honeymoon," she said.

"So did I," Liam said. "And Noah's getting married this morning. Then again, that's his bride, Holly, helping Seth and Hannah."

"So they're skipping the tradition of not seeing each other the day of the wedding?" she asked.

His laugh was husky with emotion. "Looks like it."

It looked like the threat was over as one by one, Imposters were disarmed, unmasked and handcuffed.

"Hannah and Seth are taking down the Imposter network online," Kelly said. "They're gathering data of who each Imposter is in real life, so local law enforcement can round them up."

Liam breathed a prayer of thanks. "Well, we've got some of the best law-enforcement people I know in the room to help with that. Wouldn't be surprised if warrants are issued before they even leave the barn."

"I encouraged Hannah that she and Renner should come forward, face the consequences and admit she's the one who hacked the code," Kelly said.

"Considering Holly's history with the military, as a former whistleblower, she's the right person to help them with that." Liam watched the scene unfolding for a few more moments. Then he gestured to a young man kneeling over some of the wounded Imposters, joined by a second who was helping carry the Imposter that Liam had shot outside in the snow.

"That's Trent's brother Nick, who's also a corporal, and his other brother, Max. He's a paramedic," Liam said. "I'm glad they're here. I always try very hard at making sure nobody dies on my watch."

Liam continued pointing out people in the small and efficient tactical team, as they moved through the room, booking criminals, securing weapons and even tending to the Imposters's wounds. Then Kelly's heart caught in her throat as Renner broke through the crowd and ran for Hannah, and she remembered that despite all that had just happened, they probably still hadn't greeted each other. Renner swept his wife up into his arms and kissed her deeply. Hannah clutched her husband, his arms enveloped her and they held each other as Liam's friends in law enforcement moved around them, swiftly locking down the scene.

Then the small but mighty cry of a little voice seemed to pierce through the din, and Kelly watched as Hannah and Renner turned together in unison and ran toward Mack as he carried baby Pip through the doorway.

Liam's arm tightened around Kelly and they watched as the small family cried and hugged each other in the middle of the stable.

Thank You, God. For bringing mother, father and child back together. She leaned against Liam's chest, feeling his heart beat against her cheek. *And thank You for bringing Liam back to me.*

"Come with me," Liam said. He stepped

back and grabbed her hand. "Just for a moment, please. Unless you want to stay with Renner and Hannah?"

She looked over at the small and elated family.

"Nah, I think they're good without me, right now," she said. "I'll talk to them later."

Hannah and Renner were going to have to make some difficult decisions about their future. While Kelly would love and support them whatever they decided, right now, the young couple needed to rely on each other and make their own path. Liam tugged lightly on her hand. She hesitated.

"But don't they need you to coordinate this?" she asked.

"Coordinate what?" He chuckled. "Sweetheart, I'm dead and I was never here. Clearly a bunch of random somebodies got an anonymous tip. Probably from an untraceable cell phone, I'm guessing." He looked around the room again and his head shook in amazement, as if finally taking in the scope of all that had happened. "I don't even know how to begin to explain a random group of federal, provincial and local cops, plus some military, a paramedic and even a handful of civilians all showing up for a joint operation."

She did, and looking at the unshed tears that glinted in the corners of his eyes, she knew he did, too.

For a man with no family, he certainly had a big one.

She followed him out of the stables, watching as he greeted person after person on the way out, with subtle nods and gestures that spoke volumes. They stepped outside and bright sunshine streamed down the snow toward them.

"One of them will eventually step up, take charge of how the cover story gets told, follow up on all the arrests and sort this whole thing out," Liam said. "Probably Chloe. Normally it would be someone on my team, but Jess still has her honeymoon and both Noah and Mack have weddings to worry about. I'm not actually sure how long Noah and Holly have until they're supposed to get hitched. Hopefully, we'll make sure they make it to the church on time." His voice trailed off and he looked down at her hand holding his.

"I still need a date for two weddings," he added. "With Noah and Holly's later this morning, it'll probably be a matter of sneaking in to watch from the shadows again. But Mack and Iris are getting married on New Year's Eve..."

His voice trailed off. It was a silence that seemed to spread, thick and deep like a wave of warmth through the cold, empty morning air. Somehow she knew it wasn't a silence he wanted her to speak into, so she waited.

"I don't want you to go," Liam said eventually. "I want you to stay here, by my side, with me, as I fight my way out of whatever burlap sack has descended around me and figure out how to prove to the world I'm alive. But, if you want to go, with Hannah and Renner, I will go with you and stay by your side however long it takes to figure this out. Don't get me wrong, if it was up to me I'd stay here while the Imposter network is taken down, trust Seth to untangle what they did to my online profile and work with my friends in law enforcement to figure out how best to prove the video is fake and confirm the fact I'm actually alive. That would be my first choice of what to do." He took a deep breath, took her other hand in his and raised both up to his lips. He looked at her over their knuckles. "But I don't ever want to lose you again, Kelly. No matter what happens next, that's nonnegotiable."

"You won't lose me," she said.

A grin brushed his lips. "Promise?"

"Promise, promise."

His smile spread to his eyes until it seemed to illuminate his entire face.

"You have no idea how much I love you," he said.

"I love you, too," she said. She pulled her hands from his, reached up and wrapped them around his neck. "And I'm not going anywhere. As much as I love Hannah and Renner, this is their fight to figure out together. But for me, I belong with you. It's as simple as that."

She kissed his smiling mouth, for a long moment reveling in the warmth, the strength of his arms and the security of having him there. Then suddenly, he stepped back and a look crossed his face that she'd come to think of as his detective brain activating.

"Some things are actually simple, aren't they?" he said. He closed his eyes and whispered a prayer for wisdom and courage. Then he took her hand in his. "Come on, it's time I did this the easy way."

Baffled but trusting him, too, she followed him back into the stables. All the Imposters had been carted away and the crowd had reduced to just a small handful of people standing around talking, including Hannah and Renner and the members of Liam's team.

"Hey, Seth!" Liam pointed his finger at the hacker. "How long will it take to do your thing online to prove that I'm really me, I'm not dead and the video was a deep fake?"

"Anywhere between twenty-four hours to a few days," Seth said. "The fact Hannah and I hacked the Imposter network will certainly make it easier. She unraveled the whole system and tracked every single Imposter's real identity and location." He cast their daughter an admiring glance filled with respect. "Honestly, she did like seventy percent of the work. I know I told you it would take at least three of me to take their network down, but your daughter seriously hacked circles around me. Maybe I'm getting old, too."

Hannah pressed her lips together to hide a smile that perfectly mirrored the one on Liam's face. Kelly suspected Liam had never heard Seth give anyone such high praise before.

"Now, I wasn't planning on working through Christmas," Seth went on. "But if it'll help you get your life back on track faster, I'll be on it around the clock."

Liam's Adam's apple bobbed. "I trust you to do your thing," he said finally. "In the meantime, can I assume there's something in this place that will record a video?"

"Many somethings," Seth said and yanked a cell phone from his pocket. "Will this do?"

"You're the tech guy," Liam said. "Again, I trust you to make it work. Just point at where you want me to stand. All I care is that there's nobody else in the frame and the light's good enough to see me clearly."

Seth nodded and then pointed to a patch of wall. Liam brushed a kiss over Kelly's cheek, then he let go of her hand and stepped to where Seth had pointed. Seth waved at him like a man directing traffic and Liam took a few steps in one direction and then another, until Seth held up his hand to show him he'd reached whatever specific square inch of floor the hacker apparently thought had the best light.

"Okay," Liam said. "Do your thing."

Seth held up his phone. "It's going."

A deep breath rose and fell in Liam's chest. He whispered a silent prayer.

"Hey, so I'm Liam Bearsmith, RCMP," he said. "If you know me, you know I'm not much for words, I don't like the spotlight and I'm not big on being noticed. I prefer to just quietly go about serving my country, with a lot of very amazing women and men in uniform."

He took another deep breath and glanced around the room like he was at risk of losing his words for a moment. She flashed him a thumbs-up. He smiled and looked back at the camera.

"Two things." Liam's chest rose. "Number one, clearly I'm not dead. I certainly wasn't killed by a younger, stronger and better-looking version of me. That's a deep-fake video thing that the Imposters rigged up to wreck my life. So now, I've got to clear my name, of my own murder, and prove I'm me, which is probably going to be a bit tricky. Secondly, I'm incredibly thankful to everyone who came out and said nice things about me after you thought I died. That meant a lot and I hope nobody feels weird about it now that I'm not actually dead.

"But I don't want anyone putting me on a pedestal. Or ever thinking you have to be perfect to be a good cop. On one of my first assignments, I fell in love with a witness, had an inappropriate romantic relationship and fathered a child I didn't even know about. I'm sure now that I've just blurted it out, there'll be a lot of questions I'll have to answer about that, too. But, bottom line, I'm done hiding. From my past and from this trumped-up murder charge. I'm going to go out living my life now and we'll see how things work themselves out. Okay, thanks and bye."

He nodded to Seth. "You can put that online?"

Seth nodded. "Yeah, I can even make you sound good."

"Thanks," Liam said and blew out a long breath. Then he glanced around the room at his friends. "I figure after the wedding we can sit around and strategize something. Except for you, Jess. I appreciate you being here but expect you to hurry up and get to your honeymoon. Same to you, too, Noah and Holly. Go put on your fancy clothes and get married. I'll see you there." He looked around. "Oh, and Chloe, there's a really great provincial officer in the St. Lawrence River district named Jake Marlie, like the hockey team, who deserves the opportunity for advancement." Liam yawned suddenly and then chuckled. "Also, I might need a nap. I haven't really slept in a couple of days."

Kelly walked over and slipped one arm

around his waist. Liam leaned down and rested his head on her shoulder and she brushed a kiss over the top of his head.

"You okay?" she asked.

"Better than okay," Liam said.

"What happens now?" she asked.

He tilted his head and looked at her. "No idea, sweetheart, but whatever it is we're facing it together."

FOURTEEN

"Five, four, three, two, one—happy New Year!"

A chorus of celebratory voices shouted around Kelly and Liam. Streamers and balloons cascaded down from the ceiling of the downtown Toronto community center. The lights flickered briefly.

She cast a glance at the tall and handsome man in the black tuxedo and bow tie who sat beside her on the fabric-draped chairs at the back of Mack and Iris's wedding-reception party. His eyebrows rose. The lights stayed on. He chuckled under his breath, then reached over, grabbed her hand and squeezed it.

"It's all over," he said softly. "There won't be any blackouts, the Imposters were all arrested and their network is gone. We're safe."

"I know." She smiled.

The last week had been incredible. After all those months she'd spent stuck alongside Hannah in the quagmire of uncertainty, it was like everything had happened at once. Over three hundred Imposters had been arrested by local law enforcement all over the world, thanks to information Hannah and Seth had gleaned from the internet. Some had just been detained and questioned, but others, like those who'd hijacked the boat and kidnapped her, Hannah and Liam, were now behind bars awaiting their trials. Despite Liam's reassurances that Seth didn't need to work over Christmas, thanks to Seth and Hannah's combined computer power, it had taken less than seventy-two hours to prove Liam's death had been faked and restore his fingerprints to file. His welcome-back email from a superior officer had added that Liam would be facing a disciplinary panel regarding his initial relationship with Kelly, all those years ago. Rumor had it that the worst Liam was facing was a slap on the wrist. But he'd assured her that whatever the consequences, it was worth it to be able go through life with Kelly and their family by his side.

More importantly, Hannah and Renner had decided to stay in Canada and come clean to the military about the true circumstances surrounding how the code was cracked, and how Hannah was the person who'd really done the decoding. Nerve-racking, Kelly knew, and the young couple were still facing a lot of uncertainty about what they'd be doing next. But they'd both been considering finding ways to use their skills to serve their country, and it seemed Liam's friends would be helping them find their way.

And Liam, Kelly, Hannah, Renner and baby Pip had been able to spend their first Christmas as a family together.

Kelly glanced down at the little baby

girl, clad in a black-and-white polka-dot dress with a big red bow, now curled up asleep in the crook of Liam's left arm.

"I can't believe she's sleeping through this," Liam said.

"I can't believe they've finally agreed on her name," Kelly said. She rolled it around on her tongue. "Alexandra Maria Katrina Phillips."

"That's a lot of name for a tiny baby." Her grandfather smiled softly. "I reckon I'll still just call her Pip."

"I think I will, too."

She looked out over the dance floor at where Renner and Hannah stood, with their arms wrapped around each other and lost in each other's eyes. Whatever consequences they were facing for their actions didn't begin to dim their joy at being reunited.

"Were we ever that young, foolish and recklessly in love?" she wondered out loud.

"I know I still am," Liam said.

He leaned forward and she thought for a moment he was about to kiss her. But then his eyes darted to the side as if spotting something in his peripheral vision. He pulled back.

"Stop hovering, Seth," Liam said. "I can tell you're antsy to say something."

She turned and sure enough Seth was standing a few feet away, half looking at them and partly looking at his feet. "I—I didn't want to interrupt..."

"Just spit it out," Liam said. But his smile was warm.

Seth looked at Kelly. "I was just wondering if you'd told him your news yet, because I want to tell him my news and..."

His voice trailed off as Liam's keen eyes narrowed, looking from Seth to Kelly and back again, before finally fixing on Kelly. "What did you do?"

"I enrolled in university to finally finish my criminology degree," she said.

"Really?" Liam's eyes widened. "I'm so proud of you and happy for you."

She felt a flush rise to her cheeks. "Well, I figured it's never too late to have a fresh start at life."

His gaze lingered on hers a long moment. Then his smile quirked at the edges and he glanced at Seth. Liam's eyes widened. "Don't tell me you're looking for a career in some kind of crime fighting or law enforcement, too?"

"I'm trying to," Seth admitted, shuffling from one foot to the other. "It'll mean getting a pardon for my hacking past. But it's time for me to go legit and actually use my skills to make a difference in the world. I mean, after all, the great Liam Bearsmith called me his friend."

Liam laughed, then he let go of Kelly's hand long enough to reach for Seth's and shake it. "Well, I'm proud of you, too, and I'll have your back, whatever you need."

Somewhere out in the crowd he heard Iris's voice announcing she was about to throw the wedding bouquet.

"Go on," Liam said, shooing Seth. "You don't want to miss this."

The hacker hesitated, then he frowned slightly. "You asked me to look into who changed Kelly's witness-protection file—"

"It was my father, wasn't it?" Liam asked, cutting him off.

Seth nodded. "I'm sorry."

"No, thank you," Liam said. "Now go enjoy the party, friend."

She had the distinct impression Seth was about to say something mushy or goofy. Then he turned and disappeared into the crowd.

Liam's hand found Kelly's again. He ran his fingers over hers gently.

"How long have you known?" Kelly asked.

"Since the moment I actually let myself think about it," Liam said. "He knew how deeply I loved you and that I'd asked you to marry me, because I told him. I don't know what strings he pulled to keep us apart or how he convinced himself he was doing the right thing. I know he was very badly wounded by his relationship with my mother and wanted to protect me. He loved me, but he was wrong. He wanted the very best for me. But he was wrong." He leaned forward—so did she—and his lips brushed lightly against hers. "I've found what's best for me. Twice."

"We both did," she said.

His free hand slipped to the side of her face and he kissed her with a confidence and strength that blew away whatever they'd felt for each other all those years ago. The sound of people chanting and cheering swept around them.

Suddenly she felt Liam's shoulders straighten as if sensing danger. He let go of her. His hand shot up protectively and snatched a projectile flying toward them out of the air, before it could threaten her and the baby.

A ripple of laughter filled the room. She

watched Liam's face as he looked down at what he'd just caught.

It was a dazzling bouquet of white and purple flowers. For the first time in her life, Kelly saw the strong and mighty Liam blush and she felt a matching heat fill her cheeks. He raised the huge array of flowers like a shield between them and the crowd of people now looking their way.

Kelly giggled. "You just caught Iris's wedding bouquet."

Liam laughed. "Yeah, looks like I did."

"You think she threw it to you on purpose?" Kelly whispered.

"Wouldn't put it past her," he said softly. "But I didn't know she had the aim."

They paused another moment. Neither of them spoke. She risked a quick glance around. The entire room had turned to look at them.

"You think I should tell them I'm already engaged?" Liam asked.

"Are you now?"

"Well, I seem to remember asking you

to marry me two decades ago," Liam said. "And you did say yes."

"Well, maybe you should ask me again," she said.

The smile that she felt curling on her lips seemed to match the curve of his own.

"Kelly Marshall," Liam said, "mother of my unbelievably brilliant daughter, grandmother of my insanely cute granddaughter, love of my life and the only woman I've ever wanted to spend my life with, you are going to marry me, right?"

She laughed. "Yes, Liam, of course I'll marry you."

Then their lips met in a kiss and the flowers fell to the side, as they heard the room explode in applause around them.

* * * * *

If you enjoyed this story, look for these other books by Maggie K. Black:

Christmas Witness Protection
Runaway Witness
Witness Protection Unraveled

Dear Reader,

Thank you so much for joining me for my twentieth Love Inspired Suspense! Huge thanks goes to my incredible editor Emily Rodmell, who guided, encouraged, pushed, refined and helped me through every book and along every step of the way.

I had so much fun finding a partner for Liam Bearsmith. I fell in love with Liam when he appeared on the train in *Rescuing His Secret Child* and he was such a fun character to write. By my count this is both Liam and Seth's sixth book, tying them for book appearances with both Chloe and Trent Henry.

Some of you asked why I haven't written Seth a romance yet. To be honest, I didn't think Seth's ready to be anyone's husband or father yet. He appeared as a dubious character in two books before joining Liam's team, and while I love Seth deeply, I want to make sure that when he does find love, he's ready to step up.

Thank you as always to all of you for all your letters and for sharing this journey with me,

Maggie